Clara Crenshaw

Murder with Mushrooms

A RINEHART SUSPENSE NOVEL

Rinehart Suspense Novels
by John Creasey as Gordon Ashe

A RINEHART SUSPENSE NOVEL

Murder
with
Mushrooms

by JOHN CREASEY
as GORDON ASHE

HOLT, RINEHART AND WINSTON
New York   Chicago   San Francisco

Published simultaneously in Canada by Holt, Rinehart
and Winston of Canada, Limited.

Library of Congress Cataloging in Publication Data
Creasey, John.
Murder with mushrooms.
(A Rinehart suspense novel)
I. Title.
PZ3.C86153.Mx5 [PR6005.R517] 823'.9'12 73–3748
ISBN 0–03–011156–0

First published in the United States in 1974.

Printed in the United States of America: 065

Murder with Mushrooms

A RINEHART SUSPENSE NOVEL

1

Recoil

The small man ran into the big one, recoiled, glared, and apologized. Straightening his hat he continued on his way, reached the corner, and disappeared.

The big man walked along Green Street, which was like a dozen others in Kensington. Tall, red brick houses reared on either side, their roofs white with frost.

Reaching Number 49, he passed between the pillars, and mounted the four stone steps. He rang the bell.

The door was opened almost immediately by a faded little woman, who looked up at him inquiringly.

"Good morning. Is Mr. Kittle in?"

"He's just left. If you'd been three minutes earlier, you would have caught him." The woman's manner was touched by excitement. "Is it anything important?"

"It is, rather," said the man, frowning. "Do you know where I can find him?"

"I'm afraid I don't, he's been going from one place to another all day. Is it about—?" She stopped.

"Yes, it's about the great news." The caller smiled, the gleam of splendid white teeth making it easy to forget that a broken nose marred his good looks.

"It's a dream come true," the woman said, and clasped

her hands together in delight. "I can hardly believe—" She broke off again. "You're not a newspaper man?"

"Indeed I'm not. My name's Smith. You must have heard Mr. Kittle talk about a Mr. Smith."

"I believe I have," she said, "although he doesn't talk much about his business. Is there anything *I* can do?"

"There are one or two papers I want to look at," said the man who called himself Smith.

"Oh, papers." She was disappointed. "I think he's taken all of them with him. Do you mean legal papers? From the solicitors?"

"I've come straight from their office," said the big man. "I wonder if you could look around and see if he left anything behind; the one I'm after is just a formal thing he might not have thought worth taking away."

"Well, I'll see," she said doubtfully. "But do come in." She led the way through a gloomy hall to a room that could just, by courtesy, be called a study. There were shelves filled with old books, and a roll-top desk crammed with papers. A shabby rug lay in front of the fireplace, which was filled with gray ashes.

"If there are any papers, they'll be there," said the woman, pointing to the desk. "I'm afraid it's rather untidy; the news took Jerry absolutely by surprise. Usually he's the tidiest man you could imagine. He has to be, in his business."

"I can see," said the big man diplomatically, "that Mr. Kittle is obviously a very busy man."

"He won't be, any longer. He'll be able to buy his dream house!" She couldn't repress her enthusiasm and excitement. "It will be in Surrey, with two or three acres of garden—why, what's the matter?"

The big man was regarding her with pleasant enthusiasm.

"Well, well, it's a small world, isn't it? I've a friend who

2

lives in Surrey—near Haslemere. He was telling me that there are several charming houses for sale."

"It's going to be so exciting," said Mrs. Kittle. "Are any of the papers you want there?"

"I'm afraid not. I wonder if there's any chance of them being upstairs or in another room?"

The woman shook her head. "All his work is here. Often he's poring over it until the small hours. It worried me so much. Now—"

"No need to worry about business anymore," said the big man. "What will you do—let this house?"

"Well—we haven't really thought about it. It's only three days ago that we first heard. We knew Sir Mortimer was dead, of course, but who would have dreamed that we would inherit? He never had any time for us during his life, and to tell you the truth—"

She paused, doubtfully.

"If only everyone would tell the truth, what a happy world we'd live in," said the big man sententiously.

Mrs. Kittle brightened. "Yes, wouldn't we? If Sir Mortimer had always told—but I mustn't criticize him now, must I?" Her excited laugh was almost a giggle. "What I mean is, we didn't like him and he didn't like us. He could have been so helpful."

"Helpful?" prompted Mr. Smith.

"Well, Jerry's never had good health, and he has to work so hard. If Sir Mortimer had allowed us to let off part of this great barn of a house, it would have made things so much easier, but he just wouldn't."

"So only you and your daughter—"

"Oh, not *our* daughter," said Mrs. Kittle, regretfully. "I wish we had children of our own, but we weren't blessed that way. Pru filled a big gap, but it isn't the same. We were always nervous in case Sir Mortimer tried to make her

3

leave. You see, Jerry's grandfather said we had to have the use of a house as long as we required it but he left it to Sir Mortimer to arrange the terms. Sir Mortimer always wanted to get us out of here, so he made it as difficult as he could. We can hardly believe he left everything to us," added Mrs. Kittle. "Jerry *says* he's a millionaire! I can't get it into my head. *Is* there as much money as that to come to us?"

"I believe so," said the man who called himself Smith. "It should be over a million, even when death duties are paid."

There were tears in Mrs. Kittle's eyes, and her voice was husky.

"I'll just pop up and see if he *did* take any papers upstairs, if you'll wait here a minute."

As she left the room, the big man turned to the desk. Only one of the drawers was locked. He took a penknife from his pocket and inserted the blade into the drawer. It opened quickly enough, but there were only a few papers inside. He scanned them swiftly. There were bank statements, a passbook, some bills, and two letters from solicitors, each demanding immediate payment of overdue accounts—the total owing was less than a hundred pounds.

At the back of the drawer were several old photographs. It was easy to recognize both Jeremiah and Mrs. Kittle. In each of the photographs was an older man, with a white beard. These were pinned to a marriage certificate and two birth certificates; Kittle was sixty-one, his wife fifty-seven, and they had been married for thirty-five years.

The big man dropped everything back into the drawer, closed it, and stopped, as a woman said from the door:

"Have you seen everything you want to see? Or would you like the police to come and help you?"

2

Persuasion

It was the voice of a young woman, a nice voice. The big man turned and faced her. She was good to look at, tall, dressed in a tweed suit and a tweed topcoat. Obviously she had just come from outdoors.

"Supposing we have lunch together," suggested the big man. "You can call the police afterwards if you still want to."

As he spoke, Mrs. Kittle came into the room. At the sight of the girl, her face lit up.

"Why, I didn't expect you to be here now, Pru. Everything's all right at the shop, isn't it?"

The girl smiled reassuringly. "I asked if I could have the day off, and Old Roddy said I could. Who is this gentleman, Aunt May?"

"Oh, he's Mr. Smith—from the solicitors. I'm awfully sorry, Mr. Smith, there aren't any papers upstairs. Jerry must have taken the one you want with him. Shall I tell him to ring you?"

"If you'll be kind enough to ask him to call Mayfair 21345 and ask for me," he said gravely. "Thank you so much." His smile would have dispelled most people's suspicion as he moved toward the door. "If it's between one

5

and two, I'll be at Berry's, in Greek Street. I don't know the telephone number there, but it'll be in the book."

"I'll see Mr. Smith out," said the girl.

"Yes, do, dear. The grocer will be here any minute; he hates it if I keep him waiting." Mrs. Kittle hurried off, calling good-bye to Mr. Smith over her shoulder, and the big man and the girl went toward the front door.

"Thank you," said the man. "I don't think you'll regret it."

"I'm already regretting it. The only reason I didn't tell her was—" she hesitated.

"That you can recognize an honest man when you see one."

"*When* I see one. What did you take out of that drawer?"

"Nothing."

"What were you looking for?"

"Oh, this and that. Come to Berry's and I'll tell you all about it."

He opened the front door and stood with her on the porch.

"No policeman in sight. That's awkward for you, isn't it?"

He looked down at the girl, less concerned with what she would do than with her appearance. He liked the line of her chin and the steadiness of her eyes and lips.

"Who are you?" she demanded.

"Didn't you hear Aunt May—"

She said slowly, "Are you a policeman?"

He didn't answer but sensed that anxiety was at the root of her indecision. He smiled amiably, and went down the steps. When he reached the end of the street, he turned to look at her. She was still on the steps, facing him. He waved, but she didn't move.

6

About half an hour later, the big man opened the downstairs door of a building in Hay Mews, W.1., and went up the wooden stairs. The old building, now rather charmingly arranged, had once been stables with living quarters above. At the landing he stopped in front of a closed door and took out his keys, selected a Yale, and opened it. Everything was quiet.

"Anyone about?" he called.

There was no answer.

He tossed his gloves onto a small table, and went into the largest room, crossing to a window which overlooked the mews. His expression had changed, the smile had gone, he was thoughtful, almost bleak.

Suddenly, he turned to the telephone and picked up the receiver. Then he began to dial, slowly. Soon the ringing sound came, but no one answered. As he waited, he heard behind him a stealthy movement. Without turning, he glanced up at a mirror. He could see the reflection of the door of the room, ajar as he had left it. It was moving.

He looked away from the mirror, and said into the receiver, "Patrick Dawlish here. May I speak to Felicity?"

He waited a moment and then went on:

"Hello, darling. No, I didn't have any luck . . . got inside all right, but Mrs. K doesn't know much about anything. Before I could look round, the girl turned up . . . So tiresome." He laughed, and glanced into the mirror again.

The door was wider open; he saw a slice of a man's head, and the fingers of one hand.

"Yes, you're probably right, and there was nothing in it," he said. "Rumor has wings . . . Well, I don't particularly want to spend a lot of time on it, I'd much rather get back home . . . All right, my sweet, I'll be seeing you."

He put down the receiver, and waited. There was no

sound. He waited for fully a minute before lighting a cigarette and turning. The door was wide open but the man had disappeared.

He reached it in three strides, and saw the empty hall. He opened the landing door a crack. A man was halfway down the stairs. Quietly he followed.

The man who had been in the flat was near the entrance to the mews. Short and well-dressed, he got into a small car, showing a pale, regular featured face with a thin, dark mustache as he repassed the entrance.

Dawlish murmured: "Blue Morris 10, this year's model. Registration BO2 443." He returned to the flat, and dialed the number he'd tried before. There was still no answer. He was sitting back in a huge armchair drinking when a car purred into the mews. Footsteps sounded sharply on the cobbles and less so on the stairs. He put his glass down as a woman came in at the front door.

"Hello, Felicity. Any luck?"

"Not really." She came in, untying a silk scarf. "Kittle went to Harrods Estate Office and then to several shops, and Tim took over at a bookshop. The old boy seemed prepared to browse over books all morning." She came across and sat on the arm of his chair. "How long have you been back?"

"Long enough to have disturbed a visitor."

"No!"

"Yes. No sign of malice, though. He listened to an imaginary telephone conversation I had with you, and went off. Happily, I hope! The gist of the conversation was that I didn't really think it worthwhile following up the mysterious case of Sir Mortimer Kittle, and would much prefer to come home."

"How did he get in?"

"I haven't looked, but I expect he picked the lock."

8

"What else?"

"I've a date for lunch with Pru. She was about to send for the police, but I bribed her with the offer of food at Berry's. I hope she turns up. She thinks my name is Smith, by the way, and half believes I'm a policeman. Odd."

"It's all odd. I shall be at Berry's, to keep a stern and watchful eye on you." Felicity kissed him lightly on the forehead and stood up. "I hope it's all worth the trouble."

"Meaning?"

"Was Mortimer Kittle really murdered?"

"My good girl! There was an inquest. The coroner returned a verdict of death from natural causes. How on earth can you doubt the wisdom of the oracle? True, I think the police have reason to believe that several people were greatly reliived by the verdict, but—"

"Don't play the fool, Pat. We could be wrong. You don't know that the police think it was murder."

"I've a fair idea. I also know that Sir Mortimer was rather a randy old man whose money bought him many favors. There is a rumor that he had a beautiful companion to dinner on the night he died. As was his habit, he sent all his staff out, and had dinner tête-à-tête. At least, that's what the servants guess. All they saw was the tail end of an Alsatian dog. A neighbor also saw the dog, which presumably came with the lovely. The dog wasn't there when Sir Mortimer was found. Nor was the lovely."

"I see," said Felicity, wrinkling her nose.

"Also, we have a client, remember?" Dawlish said. "A little old lady of over eighty, being the dead Sir Mortimer's mother. She came, she said, seeking not vengeance but justice, and she was afraid to ask the police to investigate because she wasn't sure that her son's reputation would stand up to close police investigation. Add the unsatisfactory verdict—in effect, that Sir Mortimer Kittle ate poisonous fungi instead of mushrooms—and the shock when his will was read, that the humble and downtrodden Kittle family of Kensington were his sole heirs. It's still possible that Jeremiah Kittle found a way to kill the old boy, knowing that he would probably inherit something. It could even be that he hated his cousin enough to kill him without hope of gain. There followed the intervention, shall we say, of Pru, who is no relation but whose fortune is mixed up with the Jeremiah Kittles'—and the fact that once you and I started to look around, an unknown third party became sufficiently interested to pay us a visit."

Felicity said, "If it wasn't for that man, I'd be inclined to think the whole thing was a mare's nest. Old people do get queer ideas. I know she convinced me at the time, but—Pat, *is* this a job for you?"

"Us."

"Is it?"

"Meaning?"

"That it's not really your cup of tea. We've spent a week on it now, and Tim has helped, too. It's cost quite a lot of money, and we don't know any more than we did when we started. We can honestly tell old Mrs. Kittle that we can't find any evidence to support her suspicion."

"But we *have* found it. Evidence of intense dislike amounting, conceivably, to hatred. Also, evidence that before the windfall, the Kensington Kittles were very hard up. Jeremiah was being dunned for two amounts which would have seemed a fortune to him four days ago."

"If Jeremiah killed his cousin, it's *not* your kind of job," insisted Felicity.

"It would depend on why he did it."

"Darling, you've big crime on the brain."

Dawlish said thoughtfully, "If nothing else turns up in the next forty-eight hours, I'll drop it."

"If only I could believe you," said Felicity resignedly. "How was I to know when I married you that your true vocation was to be a policeman? That you'd always be mixed up in every crime you could lay your hands on, acting the big detective night and day? How was I to know you were always going to get splashed over the front pages of the newspapers, as another Sherlock Holmes? How could I tell that a little old woman of eighty-one would one day come and implore you to help find the murderer of her son? How—?"

There was a ring at the front door.

3

Berry's

"Pat, someone's at the door!"

"How was I to know he was coming just when I was going to kiss you?" He lifted her off her feet in a bearlike hug.

The front doorbell rang again.

"Pat!"

"How was I to know, poor sap that I am, that I was going to love you even more today than I did ten years ago?" He released her, kissing the tip of her nose. "I'll go, you tidy your hair."

The bell rang for a third time as he opened the landing door—and stood back. The man outside, nearly as tall as Dawlish, came forward.

"Having a nap?"

Dawlish grinned.

"Just like you," said the second big man, bitterly. "I spend my morning watching fussy old geezers looking through hundreds of books, and you sleep. I'll bet you've been drinking, too. How Felicity stands it, I don't know. You at home, Fel?"

"Come in, Tim."

"Waste of brain, waste of good drinking hours, waste of patience," declared Tim, in a voice of tragedy. "Pat, you're

12

slipping. After all these years when I've been your faithful henchman, my faith is wilting. You're supposed to have a nose for crime, and all you've smelled out is a nice little chap who's come into a fortune and is spending it with the caution learned from thirty-odd years as an insurance agent on commission only."

Dawlish said dryly, "You might find yourselves very busy this afternoon."

"Does your poor, deluded husband still think that he's on to something?" marveled Tim. "He's incurable! Now let me tell you the story of my morning's labors. Prudence Lorne went to her hat shop. I took over the trailing of Kittle. At half past eleven, he left Hatchard's and went to the office of the Midlon Insurance Brokers, coming out ten minutes later with a johnny from the office. They went off—"

"On foot?" asked Dawlish.

"No, by car. I tried to follow in a cab but lost him."

Dawlish moved to the window and looked out. "The man who went off with Jeremiah Kittle was about five feet seven, wore a navy blue suit and overcoat, a newish black trilby, had a pale face with a thin, dark mustache. The car was a Morris 10 new model, dark blue, with registration number BO2 443."

Tim's face lost its look of affected boredom and discontent.

"You uncanny beggar! How did you—"

"Telepathy," said Dawlish. "All my own system, too. You must try it one day." He grinned. "Actually, the joker from the Midlon Insurance Brokers was here not long before he reached their offices. He was very interested in hearing what I had to say on the telephone. When you two have finished your lunch, you might find out what you can in a mild way about the Midlon people. And Tim, try to be at Green Street by two forty-five. Pru should be back there by then, and might not be alone. Just hold a watching brief."

Tim said, "Heaven help me. So you're still going on with it. Well, well! Who do I know who knows a lot about insurance?"

Just before one o'clock, Dawlish got out of a cab at a corner of Greek Street, Soho.

Prudence Lorne appeared to be idly looking into a shop window. He joined her. The window into which she had been looking was crammed with curios, charms, trinkets, and oddments of china, all of them clearly priced.

"Like a keepsake?" Dawlish asked. "Everything on that tray's ten shillings, I could afford it. Just. What about a silver elephant? Or that bowl of imitation fruit—you never know, it might be worth thousands." He beamed down at her.

She said, "Are you or are you not a policeman?"

"I am not."

"I don't know whether to believe you. Your name certainly isn't Smith."

He took her arm and led her across the road to Berry's. Once inside, they appeared to be in another, happier world. It was small, crowded, noisy, and bright. A man in an immaculate dinner jacket came hurrying from the far end of the restaurant.

"Mr. Dawlish, we are so pleased," he said, in heavily accented English. He bowed to Prudence Lorne. "I can find the table for you—upstairs?"

"Wonderful, Mario!"

"I will come and see you there," said Mario. "It is ma'mselle's first visit, yes?"

"Yes," said Prudence, stiffly.

"We shall be sure it will not be your last. I will soon be with you, Mr. Dawlish."

They handed over their coats and went up the narrow staircase, past a large dining room, to an alcove, with a table laid for two. There were bead curtains at the doorway.

She looked at him curiously.

"At least you're not trying to stop me from finding out who you are."

"Does 'Dawlish' help?"

"It might do," she said, settling back in her chair. "I'd heard that there were places like this, but I've never been in one before."

"Lie Number One," said Dawlish pleasantly.

"What do you mean?"

"You knew Berry's by name."

"Well, I've heard about it."

Dawlish said, "You dress for Berry's, too. Don't think I'm curious, but how can you afford it when you're the third assistant at a fashionable milliners, who isn't renowned for the salaries he pays his assistants?"

She didn't answer.

Dawlish murmured, "No one else will hear us, so suppose we try the truth for a while?"

She said slowly, "What right had you to search—?"

"None," cut in Dawlish blandly. "Ah, here's Mario. What about a steak—with mushrooms?"

Alone again, the order given, she turned to him:

"Why did you mention mushrooms—in that particular way?" Her voice was sharp.

Dawlish shrugged. "Could have been because I wanted to see your expression when they were mentioned. Was Sir Mortimer Kittle a relative of yours?"

"No."

15

"Is any Kittle a relative?"

"No."

"So you don't stand to benefit from his untimely end."

Prudence said, "Was it untimely?"

"Most people—with the exception of the Jeremiah Kittles, of course—would agree, wouldn't they?"

"Would they? Personally, I'm glad he died. He could have done so much for them, and never lifted a hand. For the first time in their lives, they're free from anxiety about money. They're the nicest little couple I've ever come across. I've lived with them now for two years, and they're almost the same as my own parents. Will you please stop worrying them?"

"Or worrying you?" murmured Dawlish.

She was angry; that gave an added sparkle to her eyes. He had been right in saying that she had dressed for Berry's. Her dress was dark in color, simply cut, obviously expensive.

"I've nothing to worry about," she said sharply.

"You have. You'd hate to see Jeremiah convicted of murder, wouldn't you?"

She cried, "Don't talk like that! It's not true. Jerry didn't kill the man. He had no idea that he was going to benefit, had no reason to think he was. I don't know who you are or what you're doing, but if you want to do *good,* kill the rumor that Jerry killed his cousin."

"Then I'd have to find out who started the rumor, wouldn't I?" asked Dawlish mildly.

"You needn't look far," said Prudence bitterly. "It was that malicious old woman—Sir Mortimer's mother."

16

4

Malice?

"So Mortimer's mother spread the rumor," said Dawlish mildly. "It could be. Has it traveled as far as Jeremiah and his wife?"

"Jeremiah's heard of it."

"Not Aunt May?"

"No, I don't think so. He's always sheltered her; I suppose he always will. He won't pay any attention to it himself, says it's just gossip which will soon die down. He's so happy, he can hardly believe his good luck. They both feel as if a fairy had waved a wand, and I'm—"

"Terrified in case it turns into a noose."

She looked at him straightly, but anger had changed to anxiety.

"You couldn't have put it better. Who are you?"

"Oh, just the owner of a nose for crime. I'm known but not always popular at Scotland Yard. I've been doing things like this for a longish time now, and have one idiosyncrasy. I don't charge a fee, even to those who can afford one. I just name a charity. Have you a pet charity?"

A half smile curved her lips.

"I think I could get along with you."

"That's what my wife's afraid of. Pru, you're a minor mystery yourself."

"My clothes?" she shrugged. "I've a small private in-

17

come, and I make the best of what clothes I have. Knowing Berry's? That isn't really surprising; half the clients at the shop make appointments to come here. Thinking you were a policeman? I wondered how far the rumor had spread, and I didn't know what it was illegal for a policeman to do."

"Heavy defeat on all counts," murmured Dawlish. "Now, let's eat."

The girl seemed satisfied to talk of trifles, until the coffee had arrived. The murmur of voices from below had died down; it was after two o'clock.

"So you want me to believe that you're just interested in the affair as a hobby?"

"Oh, no. I'm working for a malicious old lady."

Prudence said heatedly, "Did she tell you that you had only to watch Jeremiah and you would find the murderer?"

"She mentioned no names."

"I'm surprised," said Prudence acidly.

"You shouldn't be; few mothers like the idea of their only son being murdered. This one doesn't mind him leaving his money elsewhere, and has only the vaguest recollection of Jeremiah and his wife."

"Do the police know what you're doing?"

"Not yet."

"Do you think it was murder?"

"Yes."

Prudence sipped her coffee, uncaring that Dawlish was staring at her. There was strength in her face, and determination. If she really loved the Kittles, he thought, she would fight for them, no matter what it cost her.

"Know anyone who might have killed him?"

"No."

"Do you know of anyone else with an interest in the estate?"

"There are several other relatives, but none of them expected to benefit."

"Do you know anyone who might benefit if the Kittles died?"

She sat still, as if the suggestion were new to her, and as if it were frightening. Shadows which had faded from her eyes came back.

"Well?" Dawlish asked quietly.

"Yes," she said.

"Who?"

"I should benefit. Jerry told me months ago that he had left everything he possessed to me."

"Not to his wife?"

"No. She wouldn't be able to manage her affairs, she just isn't capable. He asked me if I would manage for her, should he die first, and I promised I'd help in every way I could. So he willed it to me."

Dawlish said gently, "Giving you a good motive for murdering Mortimer, if you knew that Mortimer was going to leave his money to Jeremiah."

"If I knew," said Prudence.

"Didn't you?"

She shook her head.

"Had you ever met Mortimer?"

"Yes, once. I went to plead for Jerry and May. I'd never seen him before, and I didn't want to see him again. He was prepared to be extremely helpful—in return for certain favors. There are limits to what I was prepared to do for Jerry and May Kittle."

Dawlish murmured, "Yes, he had quite a reputation. Was that the only time you saw him?"

"The only time I met him. But I saw him several times, because he had his offices near the shop where I work. I don't think he ever noticed me."

Dawlish grinned. "Well, that's the end of my arrows. More coffee?"

"But it's not the end of mine. Why did you go to the house this morning?"

"To have a look at Aunt May. To try to find any loose and incriminating papers which Jerry might have left about. And to try to get a glimpse of his will, if by chance it was there. It wasn't. I suppose you're sure he made a will?"

"Yes," said Prudence. "He didn't let Aunt May see it, and it's at his bank. You won't be able to walk in there so easily, will you?"

Dawlish chuckled. "Quiver empty?"

She nodded.

"I'll fill it up for you," said Dawlish. "Either you are a wonderful liar, or you're a good friend of Jeremiah and his wife. I think that there could have been two motives for the murder of Sir Mortimer—one obvious, one hidden. The first, that someone who expected to benefit didn't realize that there was a new will. The second, that someone who knew about the will thought he or she might do nicely if Jeremiah Kittle inherited, and so will start to work on Jeremiah."

"You mean—murder him?" Alarm flashed in her eyes.

"If you're ruled out, there doesn't seem anyone to inherit," murmured Dawlish. "Mild little men like Jeremiah often have secrets, you know. It wouldn't surprise me if someone starts to blackmail him. Will you tell me if he shows any signs of being worried?"

He took out a card, and handed it to her.

"That address will find me when I'm in Surrey; the London address and telephone number are on the back. Sure you won't have any more coffee?"

"Quite sure, thank you," said Prudence. "But haven't you forgotten another possible reason for murdering Sir Mortimer? He may have wronged someone, cheated them, working them up to a dangerous pitch of desperation. How did he make his money? I just don't know." Prudence went on, "I only know that I'm prepared to believe that Sir Mortimer Kittle was guilty of any crime under the sun. I'm prejudiced, but there are some men who just strike you as being bad. He was one." She broke off. "I must go now. I promised Aunt May I'd go out shopping with her this afternoon."

Dawlish said earnestly, "Pru, listen to me. You may be asked why you came here with me, and what we said. You're to tell anyone who may ask that some days ago you asked me to help find out the truth, and that I've now told you that I didn't intend to go on. Understand?"

She nodded.

Prudence Lorne got off the bus at Harrods and walked toward Green Street. She did not notice that a man had stepped off the same bus and was now following her. She let herself into the house, closed the door, and called: "Aunt May!" There was no answer. There was a note on the hall table. It read: "Uncle Jerry sent an *urgent* message for me. I have to go and see a house near Guildford. I'm so sorry and I'll *hurry* back." Prudence smiled as she went upstairs to her room on the second floor. Before she had time to slip out of her coat, the front doorbell rang.

She hurried downstairs, thinking it would be Mrs. Kittle, who had once more forgotten to take her key. But a man stood there. He had a scarf over his face, and the brim of his hat was pulled low over his eyes.

"Take it easy," the man said. He moved forward, kicking the door to behind him. He grasped her right arm and led her along the passage to the study. He seemed to be familiar

21

with the house. Once inside the room he let her go, standing with his back to the door, covering her with a gun.

"All you have to do is answer my questions, then you'll be all right," he said harshly. "Tell me a lie and—you'll get hurt. Understand what I mean, sister, you'll get *hurt*."

She moistened her lips.

"So just you be careful," he went on, "and don't waste time. You've been to Berry's with a guy called Dawlish. What did he want from you?"

5

The Man with the Gun

Prudence couldn't keep her eyes from the gun. The rasping voice faded, but she couldn't speak; her mouth was suddenly parched, her lips sticky. He took two slow, creeping steps toward her, and in a surge of terror she moved back.

"Didn't you hear me?"

"Yes," she said, "yes. I'll tell—you."

Everything but the threat was driven out of her mind, but she knew that she had to concentrate. Dawlish had told her what to say, but she couldn't remember what it was. What had Dawlish said? What had he said?

"Listen," said the man with the gun, "I'm in a hurry."

She gasped: "I'm so frightened I can't—can't speak. I'll be all right in a minute."

The man said, "Don't make it that long. Tell me what Dawlish wanted."

Then she remembered, and words burst out: "I wanted something from him!"

The man's eyes narrowed. He stood quite still, menace in the gun and in his eyes. She was afraid, in case he could tell that she was lying, but Dawlish had been emphatic, and Dawlish had guessed that something like this would happen.

23

Her teeth chattered.

"Go on, sister."

"I wanted him to find out who killed Sir Mortimer. He—"

"Who said the guy was killed?"

"People have been saying it was Mr. Kittle!"

"That so? It hadn't got around to me."

"I saw Dawlish a few days ago, asked him to help me. He said he'd think about it. He—"

"When did you see him?"

She'd made a deadly mistake. If she'd said that she had telephoned it would have been all right; now she would have to make up something else, and the man might be able to prove that it was a lie. She hadn't believed that she could feel so frightened; there was no calmness in her, only the sickening fear which seemed to fill her mind and make her body shake.

"It was—on Monday. I'd telephoned him for an appointment."

Had Dawlish been in London on Monday? This man might know. Where did Dawlish live? She'd glanced at the card but taken in only the one word "Haslemere."

"Where did you call him, sister?"

"At his home. Haslemere."

"So he made an appointment and you went to see him. That so?"

The overbearing note in his voice told her that he didn't believe that she had been to Haslemere; probably he knew that Dawlish had been in London on Monday. Had she already made the fatal mistake? She had to go on trying, still desperately afraid.

"I didn't go to Surrey. I saw him at—at Fortnum and Mason's. We had tea. He said he'd think about it. He sent a message to the shop—"

"What shop?"

"Where I work!"

"Go on," said the man with the gun, and his tone seemed to be less skeptical.

"He sent a message asking me to have lunch at Berry's. I went to meet him in Greek Street. He said he'd like to help me, but just didn't see there was anything he could do. I pleaded with him, but he wouldn't change his mind."

She couldn't tell whether he was convinced or not. His voice rasped out:

"Doesn't he believe that Sir Mortimer was murdered?"

"He—he didn't say."

"What made you think it was murder?"

"I've told you! There's a rumor that Mr. Kittle killed him. It's crazy, but—I'm afraid that some people might believe it. I'd heard of Dawlish—"

"Where?"

Her mind went blank. If she hadn't said that, she might have gotten away with the story, but she couldn't answer the question, couldn't think now. She felt terror, and believed that it must show in her eyes. The man took a step toward her. Then through the roaring noises in her ears, she heard the shrill ringing of a bell.

The man started. She backed away—but before she was out of reach, he drove his clenched fist into her chin, and sent her sprawling across the room. The bell rang again; she thought in sudden terror of Aunt May, who was probably outside, and might be shot down; but she couldn't move, couldn't do anything to give warning.

The bell rang again and again.

She didn't know how long she had been there. The bell stopped, and there was silence. No sound of an opening door, no sound of footsteps—just silence. Had it been Aunt May? Or had someone else called, and given up waiting?

Was the man with the gun lurking in the passage?

She struggled to her feet, and as she did so there was a lively rapping on the back door. Staggering, clutching on to chairs and tables, it seemed an age before she reached it. She turned the key and the door opened. May Kittle, pink-faced from the cold, came bustling in.

"Well, what a time you were—" She broke off. "Pru! Pru! what—"

"*The door!*" whispered Prudence.

Mrs. Kittle slammed it shut. Her hands were shaking. "Pru, what is it? What's happened? Your chin—" She turned on the tap, splashed water into a glass, and held it out. Pru lifted it to her swollen mouth. Over the rim she saw a man appear at the kitchen window. She screamed and dropped the glass.

"*Pru!*" shrieked Mrs. Kittle.

The handle of the back door turned. "There's nothing to worry about," the man said easily. He carried no gun and his cheerful face was uncovered. "I'm here to help."

"There was—a man. He—"

"He's just gone," said the stranger. "I saw him before I nipped round here. Didn't like the way he ran out of the house, and thought he might be a burglar or something. Did he give you that bruise on the chin?"

There was reassurance in his manner; he even managed to soothe Mrs. Kittle.

"I'll just go over the house for you and see that no one's lurking around."

When he returned, Mrs. Kittle was excitedly pouring boiling water into a teapot.

"We've never had a burglar, *never*. I don't know what Jerry will say, it will be such a shock. We've *never* had a burglar."

"You'll be all right," said the strange man. "I've sent for the police. You won't mind if I dodge off before they come, will you?" Behind Mrs. Kittle's back, his lips formed the word *"Dawlish."* Quietly he withdrew, making little sound but for the closing of the front door. He might almost have been a figment of the imagination, yet he left both women calmer.

Mrs. Kittle picked up a cup of steaming tea and handed it unsteadily to Prudence.

"We don't even know his *name,* Pru. Oh, what a shock it was. I nearly didn't get back in time. I didn't like the house a bit, either, so I didn't stay long. I forgot my key, too. I—Pru, darling, your chin! Let me bathe it."

Dawlish leaned back in his chair and watched Felicity. She sat at the piano, strumming a little nonsense tune. Without looking around, she said:

"What did you think of Prudence Lorne?"

"Favorable on the whole, though well aware that she might have been fooling me. It's possible that she knows something she hasn't told me yet, but I doubt if she has a guilty conscience."

"You're usually right."

"Thanks. What about you and Tim?"

"We didn't do very much," said Felicity. "Tim made an appointment for four-thirty with a friend who's in insurance. Pat, are you quite sure that man from the Midlon who went off with Jeremiah Kittle was the man who came here?"

A car stopped outside. Felicity opened the door as Tim Jeremy came up the stairs, three at a time. He stopped short at the sight of Dawlish, who lay back with his eyes closed.

"Busy?" he demanded dryly.

"Preparing to be," said Dawlish, opening one eye.

"Pru had a visitor," said Tim, intent on causing consternation. "And the visitor had a gun. The man took to his heels when Ma Kittle turned up. He'd certainly set about the poor girl, but I didn't wait to find out what he was after. I'd sent for the police, and thought it better to leave her to work out her own story with them and with us. Give us a chance to find out what stuff she's made of."

Dawlish opened his other eye.

"I don't see that you could have done much else, Tim. When the police have finished at Green Street, she'll get in touch with us. The man probably wanted to find out what was said at luncheon."

The telephone rang as he finished, and Dawlish stretched out a languid hand. Holding the receiver to his ear for a moment, he said:

"Hello, Pru, you haven't lost much time."

6

Bright Young Man

Dawlish listened attentively. Then:

"You couldn't have done better. You've probably convinced him that I'm backing out of the business, and that's what we'd like him to believe for a little while longer. What did you tell the police?"

"Just that the man had forced his way in, knocked me out, and then disappeared."

"Excellent. Stick to that story when Uncle Jerry comes home, and I'll send you word. If anyone comes to see you and starts to talk about Uncle Tom Cobleigh, you can be sure he comes from me."

Pru laughed rather shakily.

"It won't last long," Dawlish promised her.

He hung up, smiled at Felicity as she went out to get some tea, and turned to Tim.

"Know of a bright young man to act as watchdog?"

"Well, you and I won't do, obviously. We might try Ted Beresford. He'd come like a shot."

"We'll certainly need Ted, but not for that. Don't tell me you haven't seen the biggest thing that sticks out in this affair."

"You're dying to tell me, so who am I to deprive you of such a privilege? Get on with it."

Dawlish laughed. "Why should anyone take the trouble to send a man to have a look round here? Why should they send another, plus gun, to put the fear of death into Pru, so as to find out what she'd said to me? Don't make me tell you, I'm conceited enough already."

Felicity came and stood in the doorway.

"I'm afraid he's right," she said. "About the conceited part anyway."

Tim grinned. "You mean they're rattled at the idea of the great Patrick Dawlish becoming interested? Hum."

Dawlish said, "Straws perhaps, but they add to my hunch that there's crime here, and that the Kensington Kittles are mixed up in it by accident. I wouldn't say it's established yet, but it looks like it. Our unknowns have a man at the Midlon Insurance Brokers, and by working on that firm we might find out who they are. There is another way."

"Police?" murmured Tim.

"Yes. I fancy that the pundits at the Yard guess a thing or two about Sir Mortimer's death, and it might be worth having a talk with Bill Trivett. We'll see this insurance friend of yours first, and then make up our minds. You're due at four-thirty, aren't you?"

"Yes. Coming?"

"Like to leave the interview to me, while you fix Ted and then take a trip to the East End?" asked Dawlish. "You could find out if any of our contacts there have any ideas."

"That suits me," said Tim, and turned to help Felicity with the tea trolley. "The man you're to see is Arthur Harrison, directing secretary of the Safeguard Assurance Company."

"How did you meet him?"

"I was chatting to him at the club, yesterday at lunch-time. No one in London knows more about insurance."

"Did you tell him what you wanted?"

30

"Just said my friend Dawlish had an insurance problem," Tim said, with a grin.

The offices of the Safeguard Assurance Company were in Leadenhall Street, where London's financial barons brood in drab gray buildings in that district known as "the City," huddled together as if to defend themselves against attacks upon their possessions and their power.

Mention of Arthur Harrison won immediate respect. Dawlish was taken across a marble hall to a sumptuous elevator. He went up to the third floor, and was led along a carpeted passage with walnut paneled walls. A room at the end was marked *Directing Secretary—Inquiries.* Beyond was a waiting room, with large and luxurious armchairs.

Here a prim, middle-aged woman took him in charge.

"Mr. Harrison is expecting you, Mr. Jeremy."

Another door opened, and he was in the inner sanctum. Behind an imposing desk sat a middle-aged man with sharp features and the bulging eye of a predatory fish. By his side stood a younger man with hair so fair that it was almost white.

"Mr. Jeremy, Mr. Harrison," said the prim woman, and disappeared silently across the thick carpet.

"Tim sent me as a substitute, he couldn't make it," Dawlish said pleasantly. "I'm Patrick Dawlish."

Harrison smiled. "When he said that he was puzzled by some of the activities of the Midlon concern, and you had an insurance problem, I read between the lines," he said easily. He turned to the young man. "This is Mr. Renfrew, who is on our staff. His particular line is to inquire into claims made against insurance policies whenever there appears to be anything dubious about them."

"How do you do," said Dawlish. "Do you often get swindled?"

"Now and again. At the moment it is the Midlon setup which is chiefly interesting me."

"Bad reputation?" inquired Dawlish.

"Well, let us say, curious associations."

"I'm not going to ask what they are at this stage," said Dawlish. "Before we go on further, shall we see if I'm anywhere near the mark about the kind of life an insurance broker leads? He is a man who acts as middleman between you and the man or company that wants insurance? He deals with all the companies, large and small, knowing which of them will give the best deal for this, that, or the other type of insurance and assurance?"

"That is about right," said Harrison.

"The broker gets a commission from the insurance company, not from the client," Dawlish hazarded.

"He may also get a payment from the insured, if he gets terms more advantageous than the insured was getting before. There's no legal rule as to what profit or reward a broker can get."

"Are most of them pretty reputable?"

"Oh, yes. We do a great deal of business with brokers, most companies do. Rumors about a brokerage firm's reputation could soon put it out of business. They're experts, they specialize, and they introduce a great deal of business. Often they can advise the insured better than we can—we want to sell our own insurance, after all! Each company has its own advantages to offer, and the broker covers them all. Midlon is a comparatively small and new company which has done some extremely good business. We have no complaint against them, but—" Harrison leaned back and pressed the tips of his fingers together— "many of the companies whose business they handled were controlled in part or wholly by Sir Mortimer Kittle."

Dawlish's face remained blankly innocent.

"The man who ate the fungi? I see. As he's gone, you wonder whether Midlon will change its policy. Is that all?"

Harrison and Renfrew exchanged glances.

"Not quite all," said Harrison. "The facts are freely available, there is no reason why we should hide them. This company recently concluded agreements for many substantial insurances against fire. There have been three claims. Each, of course, was closely investigated but there was no sign of arson. The claims have been met in full. Yet three in fairly quick succession naturally aroused some interest."

"Why not say suspicion?" murmured Dawlish.

"We can't prevent you from guessing. Midlon has prospered, and has served us well in spite of these incidents, yet we are naturally curious about your interest. Have you any reason to believe that all isn't well there?"

"Not yet," said Dawlish. "The firm's cropped up in a little problem I'm trying to solve."

"The murder of Sir Mortimer Kittle?"

Dawlish smiled amiably.

"Need we fence?" asked Harrison mildly.

"Alas, we need," said Dawlish. "There is such a thing as a law of slander. But I'll make a suggestion. I'm very interested in big fires. Indulge my interest and consult me about these you've mentioned. Let me work with Mr. Renfrew, he as your investigator, I as the consultant. We can then talk in confidence under conditions of professional secrecy, as it were. Of course, I might advise Mr. Renfrew to do certain things which wouldn't normally come under his control, but you know what professional consultants are like."

Harrison murmured, "That could be arranged."

"But I must be fair," said Dawlish, "and put certain facts before you. I was talking to a young woman on this same problem only this morning, and she was grievously as-

33

saulted an hour afterwards. I was followed from my London flat this afternoon, but managed to elude the chap. So Mr. Renfrew and I would have to meet in secret, and he might find himself eating the wrong kind of mushrooms."

Harrison leaned forward.

"You take a grave view, Mr. Dawlish."

"Very."

"If you really think that violence might occur, the police—"

"Will have to be consulted. I'm seeing Trivett of the Yard after I leave here," said Dawlish. "We've worked together before. I think he'll play, but in some things it's better to do without the police, and occasionally they're quite willing to turn a blind eye. Believe me, they'll be just as eager to get to the bottom of any insurance racket as you are."

"I shall want a little time to think this over," said Harrison. "Supposing Mr. Renfrew telephones you this evening. By eight o'clock, shall we say?"

7

Trivett

Two policemen on duty at the big white building which housed the Criminal Investigation Department saluted Dawlish as he went inside.

Superintendent William Trivett was in his office and would be pleased to see Mr. Dawlish.

Dawlish walked through the wide, stone passages and went up in the self-operated elevator, conscious of nostalgia, of a tightening of his nerves which came whenever he visited this home of cold, ruthless investigation. He had often been here; had talked with, argued with, and occasionally almost fought with, Yard men. He had one firm friend among them: Bill Trivett. Between them there was sympathy and understanding, and the Yard authorities gave facilities to Dawlish forbidden to most.

Good-looking, keen-eyed, Trivett rose now to greet Dawlish.

"The very chap I was expecting. Sit down, Pat. I wondered how long it would be before you came and asked for help."

"Asked? Or offered?"

Trivett pushed cigarettes across his large, tidy desk.

"Is it Kittle?"

"Just a hunch," murmured Dawlish. "You're right, though. It is Kittle."

Trivett smiled. "What's your angle?"

"Sir Mortimer's mother thinks he was murdered."

"The old woman?" Trivett looked surprised. "She gave no inkling to me."

"Dare I ask why you went personally to see her?"

Trivett hesitated. "Let's put it this way, Pat. Sir Mortimer Kittle was a millionaire, and had a lot of business interests. We still don't know how far those interests spread. He was a minor dictator, a brilliant financier, and a strong personality. Everyone connected with his companies did what he told them. Some of the companies were in a bad way. Since his death, the bottom's dropped out of the market of many." Trivett shrugged. "Others might start to drop."

"Hmm," murmured Dawlish. "That makes two avenues for exploration."

"Two?"

"I've just come from the Safeguard offices. They're likely to do the oddest thing, Bill—even consult me on this and that. Mysterious fires, heavy claims paid out."

"I knew they were interested." Trivett chuckled. "If you've got your foot in there, you can go to a lot of places you couldn't on your own. It's not a bad idea."

"Meaning," said Dawlish, "that you won't object if I make a few inquiries."

"All strictly within the law."

"Oh, of course!"

Trivett said dryly, "Until it suits you to go outside it. Pat, I don't *know* anything. That verdict stands and I can't upset it, however odd I might think the setup to be. While it's true that Mortimer Kittle had a fortune in gilt-edged, he also held a controlling interest in industrial companies which have suffered. Most of the other shares in these were held

36

by little people. They'll all be badly knocked by any loss, and a lot of them may panic into selling. It could all be quite open and aboveboard, but—" He broke off, shrugging.

Dawlish said dryly, "Had any interesting reports from Kittle relatives lately?"

Trivett frowned. "What do you know about that?"

"Tim was watching Green Street, and there was a bit of a rumpus."

"I know it's a waste of time talking to you, but don't start being too clever on this affair, Pat." Trivett was serious. "If you know anything more than you've said, pass it on."

"That's why I'm here," said Dawlish, blandly. "Prudence Lorne had lunch with me, and was afterwards attacked. Whether by someone who thought that Jeremiah Kittle had a million pounds tucked away in his desk, or whether because I was showing an interest, I don't know. Bill—"

"Yes?"

"Cards on the table. Have you any idea who and what is behind all this?"

"I can't even be sure that anything or anyone is," said Trivett. "I just don't like it, and I'm not convinced that Sir Mortimer Kittle died of fungi poisoning. Or if he did, that it was accidental."

"Any slant on the Kensington Kittles?"

Trivett shrugged. "It's almost impossible to suspect them of having any part in it. They certainly had no opportunity. They hadn't seen their cousin for years. The poison was taken sometime between four o'clock in the afternoon and eight-thirty in the evening. According to the servants, there was a woman guest for dinner. The servants were sent packing. We've no idea who the woman was, but someone went there with an Alsatian dog. It was seen by a neighbor, and we've found and identified hairs which are undoubt-

37

edly from an Alsatian. That's all. The Kensington Kittles were having tea with some friends and went to the cinema with them afterwards. It's just conceivable that Jeremiah is much more cunning than we think, but—"

"Reason argues against it," said Dawlish. "Well, we both start from scratch. Except that someone who knows I've been prodding doesn't like the idea."

Trivett looked up at him steadily.

"I see. Be careful. And don't keep too much to yourself." He didn't seem to think that the advice would go very deep.

Replete and at peace, Dawlish finished supper and prepared to read the latest political extravaganza of a distinguished diplomat.

The flat was a pied-à-terre which they had rented a few months before. They used it whenever they were in London; but they did not use it alone. Friends, relatives, even acquaintances of short standing begged shelter in it from the fierce hunt to find hotel rooms at short notice. He was hardly surprised when the doorbell rang.

Felicity gave a grimace of resignation and rose to answer it. As she reached the door, the telephone began to ring. The noise was not enough to deaden the voices in the hall.

"Is Mr. Dawlish in?"

"I think so. Who are you, please?"

"My name is Charles Renfrew."

Dawlish frowned and put the receiver down on the table. He was most interested to know why Renfrew had called in person instead of telephoning.

Felicity came in and closed the door softly.

"I heard," said Dawlish. "Have a look outside, will you, and report any lurking strangers."

She went out, without a word, and Dawlish picked up the receiver.

"It's Pru isn't it? What's the trouble?"

Prudence said, "Mr. Dawlish, have you heard from Mr. Kittle?" Her voice was breathless.

"No. Why should I hear from him?"

"He isn't back. He's always punctual, and he said he would be here by six. Now it's nearly eight o'clock. Mrs. Kittle is afraid that something might have happened to him after the burglary."

"It's not likely," Dawlish said untruthfully. "I shouldn't worry; he'll turn up."

"Do you think we ought to go to the police?"

"Not yet," said Dawlish. "I'll see to that."

A few minutes later he put the receiver down, and looked at the door. Kittle might be missing; it was too early to jump to conclusions, but that couldn't be ruled out. The wise thing was to call Trivett. But other things pressed, chiefly Renfrew and his personal call. If Renfrew were going to throw his weight about, ignoring advice, it would be impossible to work with him. Renfrew would be very different from Tim and Ted, whose eager cooperation Dawlish was inclined to take for granted.

Ten minutes wouldn't make any difference to Kittle. It was now eight o'clock. At ten minutes past he would call the Green Street house, and if Kittle hadn't returned, inform the police. Listening intently, he could hear no sound. Gently he opened the door.

The hall was empty.

He grinned, suspecting Renfrew of snooping, and then heard a cry which sent everything else out of his mind.

It was Felicity's voice, and she called his name as if she were desperately afraid.

The cry came from the mews, not the foot of the stairs. The light here was poor, shroudy, menacing. Dawlish turned and raced down. As he went out of the open front door, someone stuck out a foot and he crashed to the ground.

8

Fracas

Dawlish hit the cobbles. The fall didn't stun or wind him, and he shot out a hand to grab his assailant's ankle. A heavy blow caught him on the shoulder but he hung on until, wildly staggering, the man fell.

A car engine hummed.

Footsteps thudded down the stairs inside, and Renfrew cried out, "What's up?" Dawlish got to his feet, seeing the car moving out of the mews, its red taillights glowing. He was vaguely aware of scuffling behind him as he reached the entrance of the mews. The car had turned right, heading toward Park Lane. He raced toward it, trying to focus his gaze on the registration number; he read BO2, and then the front and rear lights went out. The car swung around the corner.

Dawlish roared *"Police!"* but it was no use; he could save his breath.

The car turned into the stream of traffic, toward Hyde Park Corner. Here, the light was better; he saw that it was a small, dark car, almost certainly BO2 443. He hadn't a chance to catch it, now. He swung around, running back again toward the mews, and as he ran, a man loomed up.

"Daw—" began Renfrew.

"Later." Dawlish pushed past him without slackening

speed, and raced up the stairs. He was at the telephone within two minutes of starting back, and although he was breathing hard, his fingers were steady as he dialed.

"Scotland Yard, can I help you?"

"My wife has been kidnapped from Hay Mews, W.1. She was driven off by an unidentified man in a dark blue Morris 10, registration number BO2, and possibly 443. When last seen it was heading for Hyde Park Corner from the direction of Grosvenor House. All clear?"

"Yes, sir. Your name, please?"

"Dawlish, Patrick Dawlish, Hay Mews. Mayfair 21345."

"Description of the lady, sir?"

He described her briefly and vividly.

"Please wait until you have a call from us, sir."

While talking, Dawlish had been aware that Renfrew had come in. Now he turned to look at him, noticing the ash-blonde hair, the almost excessive self-control.

Dawlish said, "Where's the man?"

"Downstairs—knocked cold."

"Tied up?"

"No, he—"

Dawlish said harshly, "Make sure he can't get away."

Renfrew hesitated, then turned and went out. With a steady hand, Dawlish dialed another number, and a woman answered.

"Joan?" he asked.

"Yes, who—oh, it's Pat. Ted and Tim were just coming to see you." This was Joan, Ted Beresford's wife. "How's Felicity, Pat? Can I have a word with her?"

Dawlish said, "Sorry, Joan. No. Tell them to hurry, will you?"

He didn't want to talk, didn't feel that he could talk about Felicity. At the foot of the stairs, Renfrew was bending over a man's inert body. He looked up.

41

"Come to see that I make a good job of it?"

"Someone has to," said Dawlish. He went out, and the cold air of the night met him; he hadn't noticed the chill before. He stood for a few seconds in the light of the dim lamp placed in the middle of the archway at the entrance of the mews. His eyes became more accustomed to the gloom, and he moved about, looking in the corners, peering over the closed garages. Everywhere was quiet, except for the distant hum of traffic. There was no one hiding in the mews, nothing to show who had been here, until he reached the corner nearest the flat door. Anyone standing in that corner would be in shadow. Stooping, he saw that three cigarette ends had been stamped out, and a fourth was still smoldering. He picked up the ends and dropped them into a matchbox.

Renfrew said from behind him:

"What's happened, Dawlish?"

Dawlish said, "You wouldn't know." He felt furiously angry with the man, and tried to tell himself that Renfrew wasn't to blame; not obviously to blame, anyhow. He went in, and waited while looking at the prisoner, a small man whose head lolled on his chest. Renfrew had been right: he hadn't needed tying up. Dawlish hoisted the prisoner onto his shoulders and carried him upstairs, with Renfrew only a pace or two behind. Dawlish went into the bathroom and lowered his prisoner into the bath.

The man's dark clothes showed black against the white porcelain.

"If you're squeamish, go and wait downstairs," Dawlish said.

Renfrew took the shower nozzle off its hook, pointed it toward the prisoner's face, and turned the water full on. The streams spurted out, splashing against the sallow face, drenching the clothes. The man's eyes began to flicker.

42

Dawlish kept the icy jets on him, and Renfrew stood by his side, not saying a word.

The prisoner's eyes opened wide. He couldn't use his hands, couldn't stop the stream or evade the spiteful force of water.

Dawlish said, "Listen. I shall break your neck if you don't tell me where my wife has gone."

The man gasped, "Stop that water, stop it!"

Dawlish turned the tap off. The bath was half full of water now, the sides of the man's coat floating to the surface.

"Where is my wife?"

"I—I don't know!"

Dawlish gripped the man's neck fiercely.

"Where is my wife?"

Terrified eyes in that small, sallow face peered up at him. Water streamed from the man's black hair, down his cheeks, into his eyes and thin, pale mouth.

"I tell you I don't know! They told me to watch. Then Kemp—"

"Who's Kemp?"

"My boss." The man licked his lips. "Kemp told me to trip you up, that's all I know, I don't know where she is."

"Where can I find Kemp?"

"I—"

Dawlish stretched out his hand again. As he did so, there was a knock at the front door.

Dawlish said, "Renfrew, be a good chap, go downstairs and see who that is. If it's the police, stall them until I've finished with this man. I'll choke the life out of him if he doesn't tell me the truth, and the police mightn't think that's a good idea."

"*I don't know!*" the prisoner screeched.

Renfrew said, "Don't go too far, Dawlish."

43

"Hurry, will you?" Dawlish waited until Renfrew had gone, then closed and locked the door, and turned and stared down at his victim. The man looked pitiable, drenched, shivering. He tried to repeat that he didn't know, but couldn't get the words out.

Dawlish said, his voice obstinate and deadly, "Where can I find Kemp?"

"I don't know!"

"We'll see about that."

The fear of death showed in the little man's eyes.

A man called out from the hall, "Let us in, Dawlish, don't play the fool."

That was a policeman from the Yard.

Dawlish knew the Yard man—Detective Inspector Hall. Hall was big, burly, with a square chin, and bright, penetrating blue eyes. His face was expressionless as he looked at the bath.

"What's this about your wife?"

"You should know. This man helped to get her away."

"I see," said Hall. He beckoned two men who were waiting outside. "Take him out, squeeze off all the water you can, and then bundle him up in a blanket and take him to Cannon Row. Tell Mr. Trivett as soon as you get there."

"If you'd been five more minutes, I might have learned something from him," Dawlish said.

"Was she hurt?" asked Hall.

"I don't know." Dawlish looked at Renfrew, who stood in the living room doorway. "I had a visitor, and thought he had probably been followed. I asked my wife to go and see if anyone was about in the mews. They grabbed her."

"And this is the only man you caught?"

"I didn't catch him, Renfrew did. Mr. Renfrew, this is Detective Inspector Hall, of New Scotland Yard." Dawlish

44

pushed past the two men and went into the living room. He knew that he was in no frame of mind to talk to Renfrew or the police; he would have to get a grip on himself or he'd do something he'd regret. Renfrew was still the target of his anger, but justice was stirring. He couldn't be sure that he was even partly to blame.

Hall said from the door:

"I'll be leaving a man outside, and we'll have a good look round, of course. There might be word any minute, the patrols—"

The telephone rang.

9

News of a Kind

Dawlish's hand was quite steady as he lifted the receiver. Renfrew and Hall came into the room, moving silently.

"Dawlish speaking."

"I thought I ought to ring you at once," said Prudence Lorne. "We've had a message from Mr. Kittle."

"That's fine. Where is he?"

"He's had to go to Manchester," said Prudence. "He telephoned Aunt May—apparently it's important business. You haven't told the police anything, have you?"

"No," said Dawlish.

"That's good—Aunt May is terrified of them coming again." Prudence's laugh was a little high-pitched; was it imagination, or was she being too emphatic? "There's another thing, don't worry about sending anyone here tonight. We're just off to bed. I feel much safer now."

"You've nothing to worry about," said Dawlish. "I'll keep Uncle Tom Cobleigh away for the night."

"Thanks so much. Good night."

"Good night." Dawlish put down the receiver and looked at the two men.

"News of a kind," he said. "Hall, you ought to know that Jeremiah Kittle hasn't gone home tonight, but says that business has kept him in Manchester. That means there's no man at the Kensington house. Tell Trivett, will you?"

"Yes," said Hall, and added awkwardly, "We'll do everything we can."

Dawlish said easily, "I know you will. Thanks. The prisoner talked about a Mr. Kemp and I think Kemp's known to the Midlon Insurance Broker crowd. It could be a line."

"We'll check it."

Hall went out, and the front door closed. Renfrew didn't move. A car started up in the mews and drove off; it left a heavy silence. Dawlish's face was blank as he stared into Renfrew's light gray eyes.

"Why blame me?" Renfrew asked abruptly.

"Why come in person when I asked you to telephone?"

"I shook off the man who was following me. Do you think I'm new to this game?" Renfrew's voice was abrupt, though without resentment. "I know you're good, but there's room for others in the business."

"Plenty of room," said Dawlish. "You shook your man off, but you didn't shake off the other who was in the mews, watching to see who called here."

"He'd never recognize me," Renfrew said.

Dawlish took his cigarette from his mouth and looked at the glowing tip. He seemed to be deliberating. Renfrew, with his trick of standing absolutely still, so that he was almost unnoticed, watched the big man thoughtfully.

Dawlish said, "I don't think you and I are going to get along very well, Renfrew."

"I don't see why not," Renfrew said.

"I make a lot of mistakes," said Dawlish. "That's why I recognize them so quickly in others. Supposing we meet again tomorrow? I might feel more human by then. Or had you come to report that Harrison had refused to consult the oracle?"

47

"Harrison is prepared to play."

"Telephone me in the morning," said Dawlish.

"All right," said Renfrew. He turned and went to the door, moving easily, almost lazily.

Dawlish looked at his watch; it was nine fifteen. He stared across at the piano, and could picture Felicity sitting there, playing the nonsense tune. He pictured her jumping up and coming across to him, could almost feel her as he pulled her to his knee.

He sat there for ten minutes before he heard a car turn into the mews. By the time the new callers had reached the landing, he had opened the door. Tim Jeremy's tread was light, Ted Beresford's uneven. He had an artificial leg, and trod less heavily with that than with his good one. The lamp from the hall shone on his dark, unruly hair and his ugly face. But it was attractive ugliness.

"Hello, Pat! Nice to be at work again."

Tim said, "Joan had a nonsense notion that things weren't too good."

Dawlish didn't answer. Beresford stopped smiling, and Jeremy pulled at his underlip.

These three had worked together for over ten years, had shared triumph, failure, anxiety, fear, and desperation. Ten years ago, they had been more buoyant, more carefree; life had been spiced by sorties into the strange, dark underworld of crime. Now, they were more sober in their approach.

Tim closed the door. He said sharply:

"Where's Felicity?"

"Out, and not by invitation. They snatched her from under my nose. Quick, neat, and effective. Make mine a double whiskey, will you?"

Neither of the others spoke. As they drank, Dawlish told them briefly what had happened, etching in Renfrew's

48

passive part. When he had finished, they knew as much as he; and they knew that he had been right from the beginning, when he had sensed that there was much more in the death of Sir Mortimer Kittle than had appeared on the surface.

Ted drained his pewter tankard, putting it down with a bang.

"No line to follow?"

"No direct line to Felicity. This is one time when we have to hope that the police can do a smart job. But if the police were going to stop that car, they'd have done so by now. I'm afraid Mr. Kemp has a bunk hole, and got to it before the car was seen. Probably it had false number plates; the police couldn't stop every Morris 10 in London." He clicked his finger against his empty glass, bringing a clear, ringing sound which faded gradually into silence.

"Well, we can't just stay here," said Ted.

Dawlish smoothed down his hair. "There is one simplification. We needn't try to hide ourselves any more. They know we're in it—curious how they became so certain all of a sudden. Prudence says she fooled them, and Renfrew—damn it," he went on, as if talking to himself, "Renfrew's well in with Safeguard; he can't be in this racket."

Tim said, "It's hardly likely."

"It's no more unlikely than Jeremiah Kittle," Dawlish said, "but I suppose the unlikely's the most likely thing in this business. I'd feel better if there were something to do. Tim—take over at the Kensington Kittles, will you? The police might be watching the house, but I'd feel happier if you were around. Ted, how would you like to come with me on a wild goose chase to Manchester?"

"But Kittle might be anywhere in the British Isles," Tim protested. "If they've snatched him, too, and made him send a reassuring message, they'd hardly say that he was in

49

Manchester if he really was. Even if he were there," Tim went on reasonably, "what chance would you have of finding him? Not one in a million."

Dawlish said, "I know, but I'm going."

"It's crazy. Work it out, Pat. The man who came here this morning was probably Kemp. The prisoner said that Kemp was here tonight. Kemp went off with Jeremiah, and is back in London, so he and Jeremiah probably stayed somewhere in London. The Manchester talk is all my eye—forget it."

Dawlish said doggedly, "There's a midnight train, I think."

Ted gave a rueful grin. "Count me in."

Tim shrugged. "If this hunch comes off, I'll never argue with you again."

Trivett telephoned at half past ten. There was no news of Felicity, and the small blue car with the number BO2 443 had not yet been traced. The prisoner, Horace Minney, was an old lag who had been inside half a dozen times, mostly for burglary. He stuck to his story that he did odd jobs for a man named Kemp, but always met Kemp by appointment. His description of Kemp fitted Tim's description of the man who had gone with Jeremiah Kittle from the Midlon offices.

Ted Beresford looked up at the clock at Euston Station and yawned. "Well, we're in plenty of time, but I bet we can't get sleepers."

"Worth trying," said Dawlish. "Fix corridor corner seats if you've no luck." His voice was normal, but Beresford knew that he wasn't thinking about what he was saying. "I'll be near the entrance to the platform, and won't board the train until the last minute."

The hands of the clock pointed to five minutes to eleven as Dawlish walked quickly to the barrier, for Platform 12.

50

Five people were standing waiting, to be sure of seats; he recognized none of them. Dawlish walked back. The big bookstall at the end of the platform was closed and in semidarkness. He stood, watchfully, in the depths of its shadow.

After ten minutes, Beresford came in sight, with a porter and their two cases. Soon the train was shunted in, and a dozen people crowded up. By half past eleven, a hundred or more people had boarded the train, and there was now a constant stream through the barrier.

Dawlish stood there smoking cigarette after cigarette.

At twenty-five to twelve a man and a woman came through, the woman slightly taller than her companion. The haze, the poor light, made it difficult to see her well, but she made an immediate impression; she was attractive and out of the ordinary. She wore a luxurious mink coat, and although it was impossible to see whether she was young or old, Dawlish put her down as being young.

The man who followed her looked remarkably like the man who had left Dawlish's flat and driven off, that morning. His face was pale and shadowed by the big collar of his overcoat, which was turned up. But he had no mustache.

Nevertheless, Dawlish felt his nerves tingling.

He had only seen Kemp walk for a few paces, but that walk was unusual, with a little spring each time he came up on his toes. Dawlish was almost sure it was the same man.

The couple walked along the platform and entered a sleeping car. Dawlish stayed where he was until three minutes before the train was due to start. Guards were already calling *"Close the doors, please,* only passengers on the train." Half a dozen people rushed through the barrier and along the platform—and as Dawlish drew level with the last one, he saw that it was Renfrew.

10

Night Journey

Renfrew ran toward the train, jumping into the first open door. A guard blew his whistle.

Dawlish dashed past the shouting guards. A man by an open window, seeing him coming, opened the door and dragged him in.

"A near thing."

"Yes. I don't usually leave it as late as this."

They exchanged smiles, then Dawlish moved along the narrow corridor. He glanced into each compartment but saw no sign of Renfrew.

Suddenly he caught a glimpse of the man ahead of him, passing from one coach to another. They came to the sleeping car.

Renfrew passed through. The next coach was first class. Renfrew went into one of the compartments. When Dawlish passed, he was putting his small valise onto the luggage rack. There was only one empty seat, and Renfrew was about to take it. It looked as if he had simply made for the front part of the train, not for any particular place. A little further on, Dawlish came upon Beresford ensconced in a corner seat, a case filling the one opposite him. The compartment was empty but for a middle-aged man sitting back with his eyes closed, and an expensively dressed girl, who was pretending to look at a glossy magazine while actually staring at Beresford's rugged profile.

Dawlish dropped into the seat opposite Beresford, and saw the girl looking at him over the top of the magazine, ready at any moment to plunge into conversation.

"Seen anyone we know on board?" asked Beresford, stifling a yawn.

"Friends of the K's, I think," Dawlish said.

"That's odd! Speak to them?"

"No, I didn't get the number of their sleeper."

"Pity," said Beresford.

"I'll look them up a bit later," said Dawlish.

Beresford chuckled. "Better not leave it too late, they'll be getting to bed." He yawned, put out a cigarette, and leaned back. "I'm going to have forty winks. If you don't get off early on this journey, you never settle at all."

The girl said, "It *is* uncomfortable, isn't it, they don't have half enough sleepers on this train, I think it's disgraceful."

Dawlish murmured a not very encouraging agreement.

The train began to gather speed.

By one o'clock, the girl had made a pillow of one traveling rug, had tucked another around her, and seemed to be dozing.

Beresford opened his eyes and lifted an eyebrow.

Dawlish nodded.

The man stirred as they went out of the compartment, but the girl didn't move. The train was roaring at high speed, and they swayed from side to side.

Nearing the sleepers, Dawlish stopped.

"Know where they are?" asked Ted.

"No, we'll have to look in each."

"And if they're locked?"

"Tap on each door," Dawlish said.

There was no sign of the sleeping car attendant, and there was a curious impression of silence, in spite of the noise of the train. The first three sleeping compartment doors opened at a touch; Kemp wasn't in them. The next two were locked. Dawlish noted the numbers and went on. When he'd finished, he hadn't seen Kemp, but there were seven locked doors.

Dawlish went to the first, and knocked sharply; there was immediate response, and a gray-haired man opened the door.

"Sorry," said Dawlish. The door closed sharply.

Doggedly, Dawlish dragged unknown people from their beds, some resigned, a few damning him potently.

There remained only one unopened door.

Dawlish tapped. There was a pause before a man called out:

"What is it?"

"Sorry to disturb you, sir. May I speak to you?"

The door opened an inch or two, and Kemp looked out—Kemp, beyond all question, although he'd shaved off his mustache.

"Hello," said Dawlish.

He stuck his foot against the door, sending Kemp staggering back.

The woman stared up at Dawlish from the lower bunk. There was no doubt that she was lovely; and no doubt, either, that she was prepared to take full advantage of it.

Dawlish shouldered his way into the compartment and closed the door. Kemp grabbed at the pocket of his overcoat, but Dawlish was before him. He slipped the automatic into his own pocket.

The woman said with a pout, "Aren't you masterful. And

54

so foolish. Now we *know* you're on the train; before we only thought you might be."

"I'm too big to miss," Dawlish said. "I couldn't get under the seats if I tried. Kemp, sit on the foot of the lady's bed."

Now he could see them both.

Kemp was more handsome than he had realized, as well as younger; he couldn't be much more than thirty. He had recovered his composure, and was actually lighting a cigarette.

"As you *are* here, you may as well tell us what you want," the girl said. "We'll need *some* sleep."

"Maybe you will need it. Where's my wife, Kemp?"

The man didn't answer.

The girl said, "How odd. Don't tell me you *care.*"

Dawlish said, "Where is she?"

"Oh, in lovely surroundings, and a house of excellent taste. You'd love it. It has every modern convenience and she is being given the closest possible attention." The girl laughed, showing even white teeth. "Pluto's very friendly if you treat him all right and don't disobey orders. Isn't he, Ronnie?"

Kemp didn't speak.

The girl went on: "And of course Pluto's so trainable. He's been taught to go for the face, and he never deviates. He's an expert at it—you ought to see some of the models we've practiced on. He doesn't *kill*. Ever. Ronnie, haven't you a photograph of him in your wallet?"

The train rocked as it went around a bend. Kemp stared glassily at Dawlish, while the girl leaned back against her pillows, lovely, tantalizing—cruel. "Don't you think it's time we talked business, Mr. Dawlish?"

Dawlish said, "All right, talk."

"Kate—" began Kemp.

"Don't interrupt, darling."

He kept quiet, completely dominated by the girl.

"We did hope, and almost believe, that you wouldn't interfere," she said. "But I was having Safeguard offices watched, and you were seen going there. Then I knew that you'd been fooling us. Simple, wasn't it?"

"Elementary," murmured Dawlish.

"Most important things are," said the girl lightly. "Let's look at this affair sensibly, Pat—may I call you Pat? It's so much more friendly. This has nothing to do with you. You didn't know Mortimer and you don't really know anyone else who's involved. There's no reason at all why you should take any part in it, and *all* we want is to make sure that you don't. So, all you have to do is withdraw. Your wife won't come to any harm. As soon as we've finished what we want to do, we'll release her. I'd love to be able to promise to let her go at once, but then you'd start worrying us again, and we can't risk that. You *do* see, don't you?"

11

Manchester

Dawlish didn't answer.

The beat of the train hammered into his brain persistently: chug-chug-*chug*-chug—chug-chug-*chug*-chug.

"You do understand, don't you?" asked Kate, sweetly.

Dawlish said dryly, "Oh, yes, you can certainly count on my understanding!"

"Shall we call it a deal?" asked Kate.

"Not yet," said Dawlish, mildly. "Kemp, have you ever wondered what it would be like to fall from a moving train?"

Kemp started, and the smile faded from the girl's eyes.

"It cuts you up," Dawlish said. "Multiple injuries, of course, but not usually instantaneous death. And if you fell out in the middle of the night along a line like this, you'd probably lie there for hours. No morphine or other kindly drug. Think about it."

Kemp eased his collar.

Dawlish went on, "There's a window open in the corridor, and a friend of mine is waiting near it. He knows exactly what to do. When you've gone out, Kemp, your ladyfriend will realize that I mean business, and she'll talk. Save yourself a lot of pain and an early death."

The girl said, "Don't listen to him, he'd never do it."

Dawlish grinned at Kemp.

"Wouldn't I?"

The train ran on: chug-chug-*chug*-chug.

The girl was right, Dawlish wouldn't do it; but he could make Kemp believe he meant to. He waited, to increase the tension, while the girl stared at him with a new, wary appraisal in her eyes. Then slowly Dawlish got up, stretched out his right arm. "There's plenty of room for a man like you to go through that window. Where's my wife?"

"Ronnie, don't talk!"

Kemp was going to talk. His eyes were bloodshot and frightened; the strain was too much for him. Dawlish knew that he was going to crack, and the girl also knew.

"Last chance," Dawlish said, moving forward.

Words burst from Kemp's lips. "She's at Croydon, she—"

The girl said, "Ronnie, I'll shoot you if you say another word."

She pulled her hand from beneath the bed jacket, and in it Dawlish could see a small automatic pointing steadily at Kemp.

Kate watched Kemp, paying no attention now to Dawlish, but Dawlish knew well enough that if he moved, the gun would swivel around. He didn't think she would shoot, but he couldn't be sure. Once or twice before he had come up against a woman who was prepared to be merciless, who would take such a risk, believing herself capable of getting away with it.

Supposing Kemp died?

There would be Dawlish's story against the girl's. Trivett would know who to believe, but the Public Prosecutor would have to study statements. And this bluff, or deadly earnestness—he couldn't be sure which—was not all. The woman just couldn't believe that Kemp would defy her. She was forcing her ascendancy over the mind of the man who worked for her, concentrating all her strength on the task of subduing Kemp.

Kemp muttered thickly: "I—I can't, Dawlish, she'll shoot me. I—I can't—"

The girl glanced at Dawlish, vicious, evil, her beauty, like that of a decaying fruit, suddenly blotted out.

She believed that the crisis was past. The gun now was pointed at Dawlish, but the greatest threat had gone because she thought the need had passed.

"You see, Pat, the odds are weighed against you. All you have to do—"

Dawlish had only to stretch out his hand to touch her—but if her finger was still on the trigger, she could shoot him before he could get the gun away. He'd have either to take that risk or admit defeat.

The muzzle of the automatic crept higher, dark against the white sheet.

"Don't go away, yet," she said, "we have so much to talk about."

"How right you are," said Dawlish. "You still have to tell me where my wife is." He took a cigarette out of his case and as he lowered the case toward his pocket, flipped it toward her. She saw it coming and drew back sharply. His hand, strong as iron, descended on her arm. The gun dropped from nerveless fingers. Dawlish picked it up and slipped it into his pocket.

She said, "You . . ."

"Most colorful, but surely a little overemphatic? Ronnie, dear boy, where is my wife?"

"Croydon!" gasped Kemp. "18, Hill Rise, but mind the dog—mind the dog!"

Dawlish closed the door of the compartment behind him, and heard the bolt shoot home. Beresford, leaning against the corridor, didn't move his position. A single glance at Dawlish brought a cherubic smile to his face.

"Got it, by George!"

"If I hurry," Dawlish said. They moved a few yards along. "I want you to go on to Manchester, or wherever Kemp and the woman go. Look out for Renfrew."

"Right."

"If it seems necessary, get a Manchester inquiry agency to lend a hand," went on Dawlish. "Don't give them Kittle's description. We don't want anyone up there to think this is the Kittle case. In real emergency tell the police and refer them to Bill Trivett."

"Right," said Ted. "And you?"

"I'm going to pull the alarm cord and jump off the train," Dawlish said. "In case I run into trouble on the way, telephone Trivett at the first chance. Felicity's at 18, Hill Rise, Croydon. Trivett's to look out for an Alsatian dog which answers to the name of Pluto. You needn't remind him that an Alsatian was on the scene on the night that Mortimer Kittle died."

"Right," repeated Ted. "Luck, Pat."

Dawlish went to a lavatory and pulled the alarm cord. The train started to slow down almost at once. He put one of the automatics into his friend's hand, then opened the door and climbed down to the first step, hanging onto the side of the door. The wind swept into his face and blew his hair back from his forehead. He was filled with exhilaration and a fierce sense of excitement. The slowing chug-chug-

chug-chug seemed to keep time with the phrase: *18 Hill Rise Croydon, 18 Hill Rise Croydon.*

He jumped, landing squarely, then turned away from the rail track, climbed a fence, and before the train had come to a standstill was walking over a meadow.

Twenty minutes later he reached a farmhouse, and pitching a touching story of a car breakdown, talked the farmer into driving him to the nearest station. He then telephoned Trivett, and gave him the Croydon address. At four o'clock, he was walking out of Euston, into a cab. At four thirty, he was at the wheel of the Bentley. He picked up Tim Jeremy from Green Street, then drove to Croydon. A solitary policeman in the High Street directed him to Hill Rise.

Approaching Hill Rise, Dawlish's headlights caught the figure of a man standing by a hedge. They passed him and two others nearby. Dawlish slowed down, and one of the men came hurrying toward him.

"Police?" asked Dawlish.

"That's right, sir; Mr. Trivett's gone along with Mr. Hall. They're approaching from the back, I understand. You can rest assured that the whole place is amply covered. Your wife—"

"She'll be all right," said Dawlish.

He sounded confident, but he was afraid. His fear increased as he walked toward the house. There was no past for him, no future, only the present with a powerful Alsatian, trained to savage its victims, standing at the door.

As they neared the gate, Trivett and Hall loomed out of the darkness.

12

Pluto

No light showed; only the wind made its rustling, whining noise, adding to the night's eeriness.

Dawlish whispered, "All right, Bill. Dawlish here."

The two Yard men relaxed, and Trivett moved forward. "Who's with you?"

"Tim. Found anything?"

"We haven't been here long. There's a garage built against the house. It might be possible to climb up there to the first floor. All the ground floor windows are locked, and the doors are pretty solid. Unless we can manage the first floor windows, we shan't get in without making a noise. Sure about that dog?"

"Sure enough not to take any chances. What have you brought with you?"

"Ammonia balls and tear gas. You might have a look at the garage roof, Pat. I'll bring my men in closer."

Trivett and Hall went off, making little noise. Dawlish moved toward the pale blur of the garage walls with Tim following like a shadow. Now that they were used to the darkness, they could make out the shapes of trees and bushes, and the gray square of a lawn.

An owl hooted, a long way off.

Dawlish said suddenly, "Help me with this, will you?" It was a garden seat, standing near the edge of the lawn.

They carried it to the garage, and Dawlish stood on the back, while Tim held it steady. Silently Dawlish hauled himself up to the top of the garage; one moment his legs dangled down, the next they disappeared and he was just a dark, crouching figure against the lowering sky.

Trivett and Hall came back, and Hall forced the padlock on the garage doors.

Dawlish whispered down to them:

"I can get in. Hand me that stick, will you?"

"If you get in, open the front door for us at once," Trivett said. "Don't try to see this through on your own."

Dawlish grunted.

On the sloping garage roof, Dawlish slipped a knife from his pocket, flicked open the blade, and slid it behind the closed window.

He felt the blade touch the catch. Slowly he eased the knife, controlling his strength, beating back a desire to force it swiftly and to ignore any noise.

The spring gave; the catch hit against the glass with a sharp clang. He crouched down, waiting for any sound from inside. None came. He shone his torch, looking for signs of a burglar alarm wire. None showed, but the risk remained. He inserted the blade at the bottom of the window, forced it up far enough to get his fingers inside, then lifted. The window moved noisily, but he pushed it up until it was open wide enough for him to climb through.

The curtains clung to his face like thick cobwebs. As soon as he clawed one fold aside, another enveloped him. Disentangled at last, he stood upright against the open window, waiting until he was able to distinguish some shape or form. After a few seconds, he could make out the door. He reached it in four strides; so it was a small room. With infinite caution he opened it and peered into the passage beyond.

Everything was dark and silent.

Kemp might have lied, but the expression on Kate's face when he had mentioned Hill Rise convinced Dawlish that Felicity was here—or had been here. He couldn't imagine how Kemp or the woman could have managed to get a message through to the house, but it was just possible that it had been done. It was also possible that Kate had lied about the dog, but he didn't think so.

Dawlish went back to the window for the stick, felt the gun and the little box containing three ammonia balls in his pocket. The balls were made of fragile glass which would break on the slightest impact and release the ammonia gas. It was the quickest way to put a dog temporarily out of action.

He liked dogs.

He went into the passage. There was a thick carpet, and he was able to move silently. He reached a landing, which showed the wide staircase, with a turn in the middle. There was no sound, no glimmer of light, but for a cautious flash of his own torch. The silence seemed to brood and to threaten. Would the enemy leave the place without a guard by night? Were they so sure of themselves? He might be running into all kinds of trouble. He had a mental picture of Alsatians being trained, in army schools, to get their man and to savage him. He tried to shut the picture out, but it persisted. It was very cold in the house; too cold.

He mounted the stairs to the attic rooms. When he knew the layout of the house, he would let Trivett in.

There were three doors up here. He opened each in turn.

One was a lumber room; the others were empty bedrooms. He went down, quickly, silently.

Four doors led off the wide passage, and he tried the handle of the first; it was locked. The second opened easily.

He peered inside. It was too dark to see more than the shape of a bed, but no one was here. The next door was unlocked, the room empty.

The fourth door was locked.

So Felicity might be in either of these rooms.

He stood quite still, knowing that the police were almost as much on edge as he; that Trivett and Tim would probably call him a fool if he didn't go down and let them in; and he would be a fool if he waited longer. He hurried down to the front door and pulled back the bolts.

"You there, Bill?"

"I am," Tim said. "Bill's round the back."

"Open up for Trivett and the others, will you, and ask them to leave me upstairs—until I shout." Without waiting for an answer, Dawlish bounded upstairs and began to work with his picklock on the first locked door. He would have been much happier if he could hear growling or whining, but kept the possibility that he had been fooled at the back of his mind.

The lock sprang back with a click, and now he was afraid of what he might find.

He didn't open the door at once.

He waited until he saw Tim's tall figure at the top of the stairs, then very cautiously turned the handle. He couldn't tell the difference between a dog and a human's breathing; but he was sure that there were two people in here; two people, or else a woman and a dog. He pushed the door a couple of inches wider open. Then he stood quite still.

There was a furtive movement inside; not a footstep,

nothing he could really identify, just a kind of rustle. It might have been caused by a dog. He took the torch in his right hand, and twisted the top with the other, so that it would show a long beam.

Tim was just behind him.

Dawlish waited, his heart thumping; then he thrust the door back, and directed the beam into the room. The light shone on a chair, a bed, and a mirror. Then it shone on two green eyes, which were coming at him, like glowing arrows. There was no sound, nothing to warn him except his own tense, waiting nerves—and the glow of green. It seemed to flame. He held the stick in front of him, like a pike—and suddenly it jarred against his hand and the wrist. He heard a growl and a thud as the dog dropped back.

A man's voice snapped: "The bed, Pluto!"

Then Tim switched on the light.

Felicity was on the bed with her eyes wide open, a scarf bound around her mouth. The dog leapt at her, and Dawlish went forward, grabbing at its lean, powerful body. He clutched it, and it wriggled free.

13

Progress

Felicity jerked her head back as the dog's teeth snapped. Dawlish saw a vague picture of the bed, Felicity half hidden by the leaping dog, and a gun in a man's hand.

He flung himself at the dog. A tooth tore into the flesh of his wrist. Dawlish felt the hot breath. The jaws snapped again as he dug his fingers into the soft, warm neck.

The loud roar of a shot blasted the quiet. Dawlish felt nothing but the sinewy neck, saw only the gaping mouth and the reddened eyes. A voice said into his ear:

"All right, Pat."

Tim put the muzzle of his automatic close to the dog's ear and pulled the trigger. The dog became limp on the instant; Dawlish was holding a lifeless body. He heard men rush into the room. Tim said something else, and another man appeared near Felicity. Dawlish was beginning to see her white face more clearly. He dropped the dog, and it fell heavily at his feet.

Tim took his arm.

"All right, Pat, take it easy."

Dawlish let himself be led to a chair; his breath came more naturally, and the sweat was no longer blinding him. He looked across at Tim's first victim, the dog's handler, who was nursing a wounded arm. Tim was putting a gun into his pocket. Trivett was bending over Felicity and taking the gag from her mouth. Dawlish saw that she was bound hand and foot.

Trivett had unfastened the cords at her wrists, and began to work at those tying her ankles. Dawlish went across to her, and taking her right wrist, began to rub it, gently. He was completely indifferent to the other men in the room. He knew that they took out the wounded guard, then came in for the dog, but he wasn't interested. The steel band was gone, he felt warmer and freer—a buoyancy took hold of him, he was almost exalted.

Trivett said, "Go and get a wash, Pat, you need it—we'll look after Felicity."

Dawlish found the bathroom. There were dirty streaks across his cheeks and face, smeared by the sweat. The back of his hand was torn and bleeding where the dog had bitten him.

Tim busied himself at the bathroom cabinet, emerging with gauze and adhesive tape.

"Lucky you got onto the place."

"Lucky indeed," said Dawlish. "Thank the Lord Kemp and his girlfriend were on that Manchester train. Ted's trailing them, by the way."

Tim said, "Does Trivett know this?"

"Not all of it."

Tim finished his first aid work and picked up Dawlish's coat, to help him into it.

"How much are you going to tell him?"

"That I found Kemp on that train and put the fear of death into him, so that he came across. His girlfriend, Kate, can be unnamed for the time being. I think we're more likely to get results if we deal with her ourselves than if we put Trivett onto her. It's worth trying, anyhow."

Dawlish grinned at his battered reflection in the mirror. "There should be excitement ahead."

Tim said dryly, "That's fine. Better see that Trivett doesn't add to it, though."

"We can sleep on that," said Dawlish.

Tim drove the Bentley back to the West End, with Dawlish and Felicity at the back, Felicity wrapped up in a heavy coat borrowed from a policeman.

Presently her hand stole into his. "Be careful, Pat, and don't leave Trivett out in the cold too long; you may need him."

Dawlish squeezed her hand.

"I've a feeling that it's going to be brief but concentrated. We've made a lot of progress and we're going to make much more."

Felicity didn't answer.

Half an hour later, she was in bed at the flat, and Dawlish was standing over her with a sleeping tablet. She swallowed it obediently, and sank back on her pillow. There were dark patches under her eyes, no color in her cheeks. He left the door ajar so that the light from the landing shone into the room. The window was open, and she could hear a Yard man walking to and fro outside, stationed there at Trivett's order.

The courtroom at Great Marlborough Street Police Court was crowded. Dawlish arrived at five minutes to eleven, for Trivett had telephoned to say that the two prisoners, held for kidnapping Felicity, would be charged at eleven o'clock at the earliest. Only formal evidence would be offered.

He waited outside the courtroom until a husky police sergeant gave him the sign that the two men were going into the dock.

Trivett, brief and alert, asked for an eight-day remand. No one appeared for the accused, and the formality was over in less than three minutes. Dawlish stepped further into the courtroom and looked around the public seats. Apart from two reporters, no one left after the prisoners had been taken out, and no one appeared to take any particular interest in them.

The next case was likely to drag on: a woman was charged with shoplifting.

Ten minutes after the hearing started, a man slipped out.

Dawlish studied his face as he left the courtroom. A man of medium height and lean build, he was well dressed and had a big, bushy mustache, matching his brown hair.

Dawlish left immediately after him.

The man may have been bored by the shoplifting case, but may have stayed after the other hearing, just long enough to escape notice. Followed by Dawlish, he walked briskly to Regent Street and entered the Regent Palace Hotel. He went to the cloakroom, while Dawlish waited in the crowded hall for over ten minutes. Dozens of men went in and out before the man appeared again.

He wore the same clothes, and the same black Homburg hat, but the mustache was missing. Losing mustaches was becoming a habit. He hurried to the door, on the lookout for a taxi. Dawlish slipped out of a less conspicuous entrance leading to a side street. Here several taxis waited in a line. One was already moving off, hailed by the doorman. Dawlish stepped into the next, and pushed a pound note through the open glass partition.

"The cab in front," he said, "I'm curious about it. Another pound if it's still in sight when the fare gets out."

"That quid's as good as mine," said the cabby, and started off.

14

Dawlish Says "Hello"

The two taxis followed a stream of traffic around Eros, then a bus cut in between them. Dawlish sat back, leaving the chase to his driver.

He was convinced that one of Kemp's accomplices would hold a watching brief at the police court, but couldn't yet be certain that it was the man who had removed his bushy mustache. The trail was worth following, and might lead to Kate.

He had told the police nothing about Kate.

Trivett's remarkable self-restraint might be significant. If he really wanted Dawlish to get his teeth into the affair, it suggested that there were aspects which the police couldn't handle to Trivett's satisfaction. He knew that Dawlish had met Kemp on the train to Manchester and forced the information out of him, but hadn't asked how. That was remarkable reticence, which might mean that he already guessed a great deal, and that Kemp might even now be under arrest, with or without the lovely Kate.

But there had been no word from Ted, who would surely have let him know had the couple been met at Manchester by the police; Dawlish thought he could dismiss that possibility.

What had Renfrew been doing on the train?

The taxi put on a burst of speed, and turned into the Strand. There were half a dozen taxis in sight ahead. They sped around Aldwych, came to the narrow spot at the beginning of Fleet Street, and turned left just past the Law Courts. One of them drew up fifty yards along narrow Chancery Lane.

Dawlish's driver went past.

"That's it," he said. "Want me to wait?"

"Yes." Dawlish handed him another pound note. The man who had left the Regent Palace Hotel had paid off his driver and was disappearing into a narrow doorway. Dawlish crossed leisurely and examined the nameboard just inside a gloomy hallway. He read:

Midlon Insurance Brokers—3rd Floor.

On the third floor landing were four doors, and on each was the name Midlon. Two were marked *Private,* one *Inquiries.* Dawlish opened the Inquiries door. An attractive girl with richly carmined lips looked up from a ledger.

"Good morning, sir, can I help you?"

"I hope so. I want to see the boss, but—"

"Which one?"

"That's the trouble, I don't know. I have a vague recommendation to come and—"

"It'll be Mr. Dean," the girl said decidedly, "if it's insurance. If you'll wait a minute I'll see if he's free."

She moved to a door behind her. As it opened, he heard the clatter of typewriters. Dawlish peered into the general office. Half a dozen typists were at work, and a man with horn-rimmed spectacles and a harassed expression sat at a pedestal desk. The receptionist was opening a further door marked "Mr. Dean."

"There's a gentleman—"

"Tell him to wait." A man's voice came abruptly.

Without a word, Dawlish strode silently through the

72

general office and stepped quickly into the sanctum of Mr. Dean.

A desk with several telephones confronted him, and behind it a fat man with a bald head. His skin was pink and childlike; but there was nothing childlike about his eyes. His expression as he looked at the intruder was angry, and perhaps a little frightened.

"Who the devil are you?"

Dawlish closed the door.

"The avenging angel," he said.

"Indeed. Then perhaps you will be good enough to wait outside."

Dawlish sat down, stretching his legs in front of him. He turned courteously to the younger man whom he had been following. "You must be most disappointed, so little was said at Great Marlborough Street."

The fat man's face set in an iron control.

"What do you mean?"

"Just a simple remand," Dawlish went on blandly, "with evidence to follow later. All the grim details of kidnapping, binding and gagging, and the keeping of savage dogs, kept out of the Press for the time being. How's Kate?"

The fat man said softly, "I think you must be mad."

"But even mad men have eyes, which sometimes notice mustaches which come and go."

Neither of the others spoke.

"Bashful?" asked Dawlish. "I suppose I can't blame you. I will explain why I am here in the simplest terms. It is to issue a warning. If you or your hirelings try any more tricks on my wife, or Prudence Lorne, I shall all but kill you. Not quite, but you may wish that I had." He was smiling, but his voice was quiet, cool, and deadly.

Dean shifted in his chair.

"Roberts, telephone the police!"

Roberts didn't stir.

"Wise chap," said Dawlish. "Dean, I'm calling your bluff. And Kate's. Tell her I want to see her, at my flat, by half past ten tonight. She can catch the 5:50 from Manchester and get to Euston by a quarter to ten."

"If I knew what you were talking about—"

"Oh, but you do," said Dawlish, "you do."

He reached the door. The stupefied clerks looked up at him as he passed through the outer office.

He beamed at them. "Lovely morning," he said.

He ran down the stairs lightly and leaped into the waiting taxi.

"Hay Mews, W.1. And you don't have to hurry. I want to find out if anyone is following me."

No one was.

At an underground station, he tapped for the driver to stop, and went to a telephone kiosk, found the Midlon number, and dialed. There seemed to be a nervous tremor in the voice of the girl who answered.

"Mr. Dean, please," said Dawlish, briskly.

"Who is calling him?"

"A friend of Mr. Kemp's."

"Please hold on." There was a brief pause, and then Dean's voice, harsh and abrupt. "Well, what is it?"

"Don't forget to tell Kate that zero hour is ten thirty tonight," said Dawlish.

A curly-haired young man in rumpled dungarees, one of Trivett's brighter lights, was tinkering with a car outside one of the garages in Hay Mews. He looked up and winked at Dawlish.

Upstairs, Felicity opened the landing door. Only her eyes, tired and drawn, betrayed the ordeal of the previous night.

74

"No house help this morning?" Dawlish put his arm around her and led the way to the living room.

"I told her not to come," said Felicity. "We're much better on our own at a time like this."

"Well, I certainly prefer your cooking," said Dawlish. He could see, and it grieved him, that it would be some time before she recovered from the shock of that kidnapping. "Eight days remand. A snooper from Midlon held a watching brief, and I followed him and told a man with three chins that I want to see Kate, here, tonight. You don't have to wait up."

"And Trivett?"

"I'd have a job to keep anything from him—one of his brighter young men is outside. Any news from Ted?"

"No. Tim's gone to Green Street."

"Trust Tim," murmured Dawlish. "Well, it's open warfare now, and I still haven't a notion as to what it's all about. Inheritance via Jeremiah Kittle, motive Number 1. Insurance racket, via Midlon, motive Number 2. Company frauds and stock market rigging, motive Number 3. Any preference, my sweet?"

15

News of Another Kind

Ted's voice came to him from Manchester like an oracle from heaven.

"That you, Pat?"

"All ears," said Dawlish.

"The first address is: 81 Ribbleton Street, Salford—that's where Jeremiah Kittle is—or was, until three quarters of an hour ago. He spent the night there. I discovered from a neighbor that he's been there before. It's a private house, the owner a Mr. Rossitter. He travels a great deal, is seldom at home, and has a lovely daughter. I don't have to tell you her name."

"Dear Kate?" murmured Dawlish.

"As you say, dear Kate. She and Kemp went this morning to the Midland Hotel. Single rooms, booked in advance. I'm at the Grand, by the way. I fixed up with a local agency to keep an eye on her, and she left the Midland at ten o'clock and went in a closed car, unaccompanied, to Ribbleton Street. She stayed about ten minutes, then returned to the Midland. The agency is Lee's, Piccadilly. Can you hear me?"

"Every word is being taken down."

"Right. Well, Kemp hasn't stirred out of his room. Renfrew couldn't get a room at the Midland, but he had breakfast there and is still at the place, watching the other two. He saw Kate leave, and presumably decided to stay and watch Kemp. He's biding his time."

"A crafty young man," said Dawlish.

"But efficient," Ted said. "I've fixed up for the agency to keep tabs on him, Kemp, and Kate, and to call me if they go to the station or do anything that looks odd. I gather from your voice that your news is good. Give her my love."

Dawlish laughed happily as the line went dead.

Harrison, of Safeguard, kept Dawlish waiting for only three minutes. The office, the luxury and the businesslike efficiency, were unchanged; only Renfrew was missing.

"If you have obtained results so quickly, Mr. Dawlish, I should regard it as a miracle."

"No miracle," Dawlish said regretfully. "Just odds and ends of suspicion."

"What about?"

"Let me put it this way. You'd like me to join forces with Renfrew. Now that I know Renfrew, I'm not sure that I should."

"You dislike him?"

"He doesn't go out of his way to be amiable."

"Don't be put off by his manner," Harrison said. "He is ruthless, efficient, and unquestionably loyal."

"Clear bill for Renfrew," Dawlish mused. "Thanks."

He left soon afterwards, not fully convinced of Renfrew's reliability, but convinced that Harrison and Safeguard trusted him implicitly.

Roddy's was less a shop than a salon. It had a narrow window in which was displayed one hat, a frothy creation which would doubtless cost a fortune.

Dawlish beamed at Prudence.

"My wife would like a hat," he said.

"Yes—yes, of course." Prudence recovered quickly from the shock of seeing him, and turned to Felicity. "If madame would give me some idea of the kind of hat she would like?"

Twenty-five minutes after entering Roddy's, Dawlish led Felicity out—having pledged himself to pay seventeen guineas for a bow, a flower, and a yard of veiling.

They strolled down New Bond Street to a favorite tea shop.

"I suppose you know she's exceptionally attractive?" Felicity said, as she settled herself at a corner table. "I think I may have been too harsh in advising you not to trust her. She looked worried."

Dawlish grinned. "Wait until you see Kate," he said.

At twenty minutes past five, Prudence Lorne left the hat shop. She walked well, giving no sign that she was nervous. At Piccadilly, she turned left, taking her place in a queue for the buses going toward Kensington.

Dawlish followed her at a distance. A taxi came alongside. Dawlish stopped it. "Pull up just in front of the bus stop and wait for me, will you?" he asked. The man went on, with five shillings in the palm of his hand, and Dawlish waited until Prudence had boarded a Number 9 bus. He hurried to the taxi, told the man to follow the bus, and was in sight of it when Pru got off. Five minutes later, she turned into the darkness of Green Street. Dawlish paid off the cab, and quickened his pace, anxious to keep her in sight. He scanned the doorways on either side, but saw no sign of Tim. A car turned into the street, its headlights throwing the girl's figure into sharp relief.

In the porch of the corner house next door to Number 49 there was a slight movement, as of withdrawal. Tim? Why should Tim mind being seen? A policeman? Where was the man Trivett had set to watch Prudence?—or hadn't he thought the need urgent enough?

Prudence wasn't far from her house now. Dawlish drew level with her, but didn't glance at or speak to her. They were only three doors from Number 49 when a man approached them.

The light was good enough to show that he held a gun in his right hand.

Dawlish leapt forward, and as he did so, a shot blasted the quiet of the street. Dawlish threw himself down as the other ran at him. The bullet missed. Dawlish flung out his right hand to grab the other's ankle, but the man saw the hand, and leapt over it, running toward the far end of the street. Dawlish saw the running man clearly, and fired low—but then a newcomer came hurrying from a house and got between him and the gunman. A brave but misguided man, he clutched at Dawlish's arm, losing him precious seconds. The fleeing gunman rounded the corner and disappeared as Dawlish flung off his interceptor and raced in pursuit.

He knew he would be too late.

Turning, he pushed past his pursuer, calling over his shoulder a request to send for the police, then hurried toward Number 49.

A little knot of people were standing on the pavement, among them, with a face of extreme pallor, Prudence.

"No, I've no idea what it was all about," she was saying in a taut voice. "Yes, I'm *quite* all right, really, please don't make a fuss." Her voice grew high-pitched. "I live here, I'm quite all right." She turned onto the porch and hurried up the four steps, unlocked the door, and went in.

Fifteen minutes later, Green Street had quieted down. But there was no sign of Tim nor of a policeman who, it proved, should have been watching the street.

The police car had gone; the night was dark and quiet, with a hint of fog in the air. Dawlish glanced at his watch, and the luminous dial showed twenty minutes past six.

He went up the steps to the Kittles' house and rang the bell.

16

Boyfriend?

Mrs. Kittle opened the door. She clutched the door tightly and peered around the edge, with the light shining into Dawlish's face.

"What is it?"

"Is Miss Lorne in?"

"You can't see her, she's not well!" Nervousness made the voice shrill.

"She'll see me," said Dawlish, insinuating himself into the hall. "Don't worry, Mrs. Kittle. What's the matter with Prudence?"

"I just don't know. She went rushing up to her own room, and said she had a terrible headache. She wouldn't let me make her a cup of tea or anything." Mrs. Kittle was aggrieved, but the foundation of her mood was fear. "I just don't know what to do. Mr. Kittle didn't come home yesterday, he sent me a letter from Manchester to say he would be away two or three days, it's such a worry after what happened here yesterday afternoon."

There was a film of tears in her eyes.

"I shouldn't worry," said Dawlish soothingly. "Let me go up and have a word with her. Supposing you go and make her a cup of tea and bring it upstairs in a quarter of an hour. Which is her room?"

81

"It's the first door on the right," said Mrs. Kittle, brightening up at the idea of a cup of tea.

"I hope your husband will be home soon."

"Tomorrow or the next day," said Mrs. Kittle hopefully. "You see, he has one *very* good client in Manchester, a Mr. Rossitter. I don't know what we should have done without him. Jerry always said that it was the best stroke of business he ever did, interesting Mr. Rossitter."

She moved away in the direction of the kitchen as Dawlish went upstairs. He probed searchingly into every dark shadow before tapping sharply on Pru's door.

"Who is that?"

"Dawlish."

He expected her to protest, but she opened the door readily enough. The contrast between the girl who had sold Felicity a hat so short a time before and this girl was startling. Her eyes, dark and cavernous, gazed hauntingly at him out of a paper-white face. It was easy to see that she was suffering from shock—or from the cumulative effect of several shocks.

She closed the door and turned the key in the lock.

"That attack was meant for me, wasn't it?"

"It could have been for me."

"You don't really think that," said Prudence, in a flat voice. "The man was waiting there and would have shot me if you hadn't been near. I owe you my life now. But you said that someone would be near, and that the police—" she broke off. "No, you didn't say anything about the police. I'm getting all mixed up."

"Is it surprising?" asked Dawlish gently.

"I suppose not." She began to shiver again, violently. "I—I could understand the attack yesterday, but this is so pointless. Why shoot me? Why should anyone want to kill *me?*"

"There's a reason," Dawlish said.

"Of course there is, but I don't know it. It was bad enough when the talk about Jerry started, now—" she began to pace the room. "Do *you* know anything? Why did you come to the shop?"

"I wanted my wife to see you."

"Why on earth should you?"

"She won an interest in the affair last night. She was kidnapped."

Prudence stared at him. "It turned out all right," Dawlish went on, "but it gave her a personal interest in the gentry on the other side. Pru, where is Jeremiah Kittle?"

"In Manchester—I told you."

"Are you sure?"

"Well, he rang from there. But I don't see what that has to do with this."

"Wasn't it odd that he should have gone to Manchester in the middle of this inheritance business?"

Prudence looked at him, frowning, no longer so much on edge.

"Well, no," she said. "If you knew Uncle Jerry, you wouldn't be surprised. He's had to fight for every penny he's earned. Business was of vital importance to him. I think he dreams about it. It's a habit to rush off to see his clients whenever they send for him."

"Did Rossitter write to him here?"

"I hadn't thought about that, but no, he didn't," said Prudence. "He usually goes to one of the London offices, and got the message there."

"Do you know what office?"

Pru shook her head. "He only talks about business in general terms—though it means so much to him. He's put years onto his age by working so hard, always ready to rush off to any office which offered him business. He collects insurance from private houses, you know, that is his main line—though he has other bigger deals, mostly through Rossitter."

"You've never seen Rossitter, I suppose?"

"No. I—"

She stopped. Dawlish heard Mrs. Kittle coming up the stairs, and the rattle of teacups.

He said urgently, "Pru, before your aunt comes, tell me what's really worrying you."

She gave a queer little laugh, and turning, knocked her handbag to the floor. All the contents fell out—purse, keys, compact, a letter, and two photographs. She bent to pick them up, Dawlish helping her. One of the photographs he noticed was of the Kittles taken on a stretch of beach; the other was of Charles Renfrew.

Dawlish opened the door and Mrs. Kittle came in, brisk and rather theatrically bright.

"You'll have a cup of tea with us, Mr. Smith, won't you?" she asked. "There now, if I haven't forgotten the biscuits."

As she clattered downstairs, Prudence turned to Dawlish.

"She'll be back in a moment. Is there anything more you want me to tell you?"

Dawlish picked up the snapshot and handed it to her. "One of your boyfriends?"

Pru said, "No, not in the usual meaning of the word. But has it really anything to do with you?"

"Just filling in a background," said Dawlish. "I have to know your friends before I can find your enemies."

"Jimmy is barely one, and certainly not the other."

"How did you meet him?"

Only his name wasn't Jimmy; it was Charles Renfrew.

Prudence said abruptly, "At the shop. He came in with a message one day, and the same evening I found him waiting outside. We met several times afterwards, but I haven't seen him lately. He travels about a lot, at his work."

"What work?"

"He's a salesman, I don't know in what business, and I really don't see that it matters."

"What's his surname?"

"Anderson," said Prudence.

17

Visitor

Felicity said, "No, Tim hasn't called."

Dawlish went straight to the telephone and dialed Whitehall 1212. Trivett wasn't in, but a detective inspector told him that there was no news of Mr. Jeremy. Dawlish looked into Felicity's suddenly anxious face.

"Tim's onto something, or Kate's boyfriends are better than I thought," he said. "Is Owen still outside?"

"He's gone, and a Yard man named Pratt has taken over," said Felicity. "He came up to ask me not to go out alone tonight." She shivered. "Pat, I don't like it."

Dawlish looked at his watch; it was nearly eight o'clock. "Let's have a drink and pretend to be normal. Nothing more from Ted, I suppose?"

"Yes. He telephoned to say that the woman left the Midland Hotel just after five thirty, and caught the ten-to-six train from London Road station to Euston. Ted's staying up there, because Kemp hasn't stirred out of the hotel. You're to call him if you want him to come back. Pat, do you seriously think that anything has happened to Tim?"

Dawlish pondered, and then said "Yes."

"What *is* it all about?"

"Crime," said Dawlish, somberly. There was a real possibility that Tim had scented a trail and gone off on the hunt, but Dawlish thought it more likely that he'd been removed from Green Street. These were desperate people, prepared to take desperate chances. Gone were the days when it was almost ludicrous to think of such violence in a London street. There were too many armed and violent men about, too many were prepared to deal in death.

Was Tim alive?

Dawlish said, "A lot depends on whether the woman comes tonight."

"She won't come," said Felicity, hopelessly.

Ten minutes before the train was due, Dawlish edged his way to the barrier, choosing as a place of vantage and cover a platform truck piled high with boxes. He watched both the people going onto the platform and those, like himself, who were waiting for the train to arrive. As the crowd increased, some of the nearby taxis began to warm up their engines. Kate might get one of these, or might enter one of the private cars drawn up near the arrival platform. The murky light wouldn't help him, and he realized at once that this was one of the occasions when he had planned too casually.

A woman's voice spoke from just behind Dawlish, so unexpectedly that he gave an inward start.

"Would you like any help, Mr. Dawlish?"

"Who let you out?" he asked.

"I got tired of being behind bars."

"All right, my sweet, you'll do. If Kate's dressed as she was last night, she drips mink, has a small hat like a puff of sea-mist, and walks like a dream. Supposing you go along the platform, and I wait here?"

"Fancy you trusting me," murmured Felicity.

Dawlish didn't see her until she was some way ahead. He was anxious. After the sudden attack in Green Street, he was prepared to believe that anything could happen. He saw a big man, not far from Felicity, and always the same distance from her; that was probably Trivett's man, who had followed her from the flat. Trivett would be told, then, that Felicity had come to Euston.

Would it matter?

As the train steamed in, a rustle of excitement ran through the waiting crowd. The surging crowd of porters merged with the passengers in a scene of hopeless confusion. Dawlish waited, unmoving, for the crowd to thin out. It was then that he saw Renfrew.

The man walked briskly past him, carrying the small suitcase. Dawlish forced himself to look away from the man, scanning the hurrying figures for Kate Rossitter.

At last he saw her.

A porter walked by her side, carrying two cases; and Felicity wasn't far behind. Behind both women could be seen the hefty Yard man. All three passed. Dawlish hurried to his Bentley, watching from the driver's seat the cabs come and go. Kate's porter stopped the next one that was pulling up. The Yard man beckoned a second—and spoke to Felicity. So Felicity was going to be sensible and share a cab with him.

Dawlish got into gear, ready to start in the wake of the cabs. Kate's passed him. Then came Felicity's—and Dawlish moved into the stream of traffic. At the same moment the door of his car was wrenched open. Dawlish dropped one hand to his pocket, for his gun.

Renfrew said, "Mind if I join you?"

They were soon out on the Euston Road, heading for the West End. Renfrew sat with his case on his knees; Dawlish drove without saying a word.

They turned down Baker Street, then into a road where two blocks of flats towered against the night sky. The first taxi stopped at an entrance to the first block, the other went past but stopped at the next entrance. Dawlish pulled up on the farther side of the road.

"Where do you want to go?" he asked dryly.

"This will do. Good looker, isn't she?"

"Who?"

"Kate Rossitter—who else? You didn't lose much time getting onto her."

"Thanks."

"I'm still prepared to work with you," said Renfrew. "Or have you decided to go on making the same mistake?"

"You said something about a mistake before," Dawlish said.

"I could have told you where to look for your wife."

"Could you? Where?"

"Where you found her."

Dawlish said softly, "And where did I find her?"

"At Croydon."

"And your informant?"

"The same one who told me Kemp and his girlfriend were going to Manchester. I've been watching Kemp for some time. I guessed that he was behind some of the trouble we've been having at Safeguard. If those fires were due to arson, Kemp arranged it. I was pretty sure that Kate Rossitter wouldn't burn her own pretty fingers, and guessed your wife was at Croydon. You were so self-sufficient, I left you to blunder on in your own favorite way."

Dawlish felt acute dislike of the man. If Renfrew were telling the truth, he had deliberately risked Felicity's safety.

"And why try to stop me blundering now?" he asked.

"You get results. We've that in common. I'm only

interested in results, not the way they come. I think you were born lucky. We could crack this case open between us."

"Nice of you," said Dawlish. "We must have a talk some other time. Why are you watching Kate?"

"Because she had Kemp under her thumb. I'm interested in Rossitter of Salford, too. He puts through some big insurance deals and also plays the markets—and he has dealings with Kemp. Put me down here, will you?"

Dawlish slowed the car, and Renfrew leapt from it while it was still moving. Dawlish heard him walking briskly toward the end of the street. He made himself forget the man who only wanted results and didn't care how he got them; but even forgetting, he wondered if Renfrew were right and he was allowing personal prejudice to force him into a mistake. He got out of the Bentley and went along to the first taxi. Felicity and the Yard man were still sitting in it.

He opened the door.

"Mind if I see your papers, Pratt?" He was amiable enough.

Pratt took them from his pocket, and Dawlish studied them in the light of his torch, then handed them back.

"Thanks. I'd get back to Hay Mews if I were you," he said. "I'll see the Superintendent about this later."

"Very good, sir. It's no wish of mine that Mrs. Dawlish came out tonight; my job's to look after her."

"Go into the flat with her and have a look around, will you?" said Dawlish.

He went back to the Bentley, reaching it as the cab started off. It was then ten minutes past ten; if Kate Rossitter intended to be at Hay Mews, she would soon leave here. He went inside. The block of flats was luxurious, even opulent. A smartly dressed doorman walked toward him.

"Can I help you, sir?"

"Which is Mr. Dean's flat?"

"Mr. Dean? We haven't a Mr. Dean here, sir."

Dawlish snapped his fingers in mock annoyance. "How foolish of me. I must have muddled up the names. A tall, rather stout man, frontally bald?"

The doorman's face cleared: "Oh, you mean Mr. Morgan. Yes, sir, Suite 24 on the second floor."

A pound note changed hands.

"I wonder if you'll forget that I've been inquiring for him. Businessmen have their little vanities and he wouldn't be flattered to learn that I'd muddled him up with Mr. Dean."

The pound note vanished into a large pocket.

"If you'd like to earn another five of those, you might amuse yourself by making a list of the people who call to see Mr. Morgan," said Dawlish. "If you know their names, good. If not, a description will do."

The doorman looked hard at Dawlish.

"You're Mr. Dawlish, aren't you?"

Dawlish nodded. They were both smiling as Dawlish climbed back into the Bentley.

He drove straight to Hay Mews, and as the car came to a standstill, the Yard man appeared alongside.

"All safe?" asked Dawlish.

"Everything's okay, sir. I advised Mrs. Dawlish to put on all the lights. If you don't mind my saying so, I think she's rather nervous. Wouldn't be a bad idea if you sent her away to the country, would it?"

Dawlish said, "You married?"

"I get you," said the Yard man.

It was three minutes to the half hour when Dawlish

reached the landing. Felicity opened the door, a little breathlessly.

"Three minutes to go, Pat—she won't come."

"Pity you didn't put some money on it," said Dawlish, laughing.

Until that moment, he had felt sure that Kate Rossitter would come, but now he began to doubt. The three minutes passed slowly. As Felicity began to smile a comforting, but superior, smile, a car door slammed.

Footsteps sounded in the mews, not one set, but two. There were other sounds, and then a thud and a word which sounded like "Careful!"

"Perhaps they had to carry her," Felicity said, lightly.

Dawlish said, "All right, it's funny." But he didn't look amused, and Felicity's smile faded into strained uncertainty. When Dawlish wore that black look, she was nervous, almost frightened. A heavy knock came at the door downstairs.

Dawlish hurried down, while Felicity went to the side of the landing, where she could see without being seen.

Dawlish opened the door.

Two men stood outside, with a long crate between them—they were breathing heavily.

"Mr. Dawlish?"

"That's right." Dawlish saw the Yard man hovering near the small van in which these men had come.

"Package for you, sir. Special order—to be delivered at half past ten sharp. Want us to bring it up?"

Dawlish stirred himself. "No, not yet. I'll have it opened in the yard."

18

Special Delivery

The crate was wrapped in hessian. The Yard man joined them without a word as one of the men took out a clasp knife and cut through the string. The box was tightly wrapped, and it took at least five minutes to get it clear. As the last layer was removed, they saw that it was a coffin. A sheet of paper was stuck to the wood, and with a sickening sense of dread, Dawlish read the inscription:

Timothy Jeremy
Born for a Sticky End Which Overtook Him
on November 12

It was cold and quiet in the mews; still with a deathly stillness.

One of the men said hoarsely:

"Someone playing a joke on you, guv'nor?"

"Looks like it. Have you a screwdriver?"

"Sure thing." The man went to fetch it as the Yard man's face, gray in the flickering light, loomed nearer.

"I don't like the look of this, Mr. Dawlish."

Dawlish said, "Send the men to the other side of the van, will you? It may be a booby trap and we don't want to risk any more lives."

Painstakingly, Dawlish worked on screw after screw, the

two men peering at him from a safe distance, the Yard man by his side. A clock struck somewhere nearby. There was only one more screw, and it proved more difficult than any of the others.

The screw came out.

Pratt and Dawlish took off the lid. Immediately on the top of the open coffin was a white sheet: a shroud. On it was pinned another card, which said *10:30 as requested.*

Dawlish straightened up. Could there be any danger in that? He doubted if there would be an open attack, now; this macabre joke was sufficient by itself. Nevertheless, it could be a booby trap.

Dawlish went to the Bentley, reversed in the narrow space of the yard until the headlights were shining fully on the coffin and the shroud.

By the harsh light Dawlish studied the sheet and the note pinned to it. He pressed it gently; there was cardboard fitted to the shape of the coffin, and the note was pinned to that with two drawing pins.

He went down on one knee, stretching out his penknife in an endeavor to push the point of the blade beneath a drawing pin. He began to lever the pin up, and heard Pratt catch his breath. The pin came out and rolled over to one side, and there was no alarm.

Pratt said testily, "It's safe enough."

"Keep away," Dawlish said harshly. He started on the other pin, with equal care. It began to move easily enough, Pratt was probably right. Then it stuck.

He drew the knife away.

"Here, let me do it!" snapped Pratt, and moved forward quickly.

Dawlish snatched his arm away.

"Only a fool takes unnecessary risks. Ask Felicity to bring down that old sword from the landing, will you?"

Waiting, he heard Felicity coming down the stairs, but it was a movement near the entrance to the mews which caught his attention. The headlights lit up the entrance—and the woman who was standing there.

It was Kate.

Stretching out his hand for the sword, Dawlish's eye flicked over Kate. Swathed in mink, she was keeping a safe distance. Would she wait there if she knew that there was no danger? Even if there were no booby trap, what lay beneath the shroud? Tim?

Felicity stood by his side.

"Go back a bit," said Dawlish. "Keep behind the door."

Felicity obeyed. Only Pratt stayed near, and he was far enough away and tense enough to show that he had become nervous. Dawlish knelt down and stretched the sword out at full length. With infinite patience he managed to get it beneath the stubborn drawing pin. He jerked it.

A white hot stab of flame shot into the air. Dawlish felt the searing heat, dropped the sword and staggered back. For a few seconds the coffin blazed like a gigantic firework, then the flames lessened and sank into a swirl of smoke.

Dawlish said, "Now we can get busy." He went forward, racked with fear of what he would find beneath the sheet. He pulled it and it tore away, bringing with it the asbestos fitting. Tim lay beneath.

Tim's eyes were closed. His hands were folded across his breast, and a single lily was held between his fingers.

Kate Rossitter drew nearer, and Felicity came from the doorway and joined her. The two deliverymen moved forward, wanting to help.

Dawlish eased his hands beneath Tim's body and drew him gently out. There was no sign of rigor mortis. Dawlish lifted him, with one arm beneath his knees, the other under his shoulders, hardly conscious of Tim's weight, only of the closed eyes so near his face.

Someone followed him up the stairs.

Dawlish went into the spare bedroom and eased Tim gently on to the bed. He held the limp wrist, seeking for the beat of the pulse, but could detect nothing. He was afraid that Tim was dead; and he felt hatred for the people who had done this thing.

Felicity took a small mirror off the dressing table and held it in front of Tim's mouth. Presently she withdrew it, then, without a word, thrust it in front of Dawlish. He stared down, and saw that there was a slight clouding on the surface of the glass.

Pratt called quietly that the doctor was on his way.

Dawlish said, "He'll be all right." He said it because he wanted to believe it, not because he was yet convinced that Tim would come through. The mirror might have lied; the temperature of the room might have brought the cloud.

From the door, Kate Rossitter spoke.

"Is there anything I can do?"

Dawlish turned and looked at her, bleakly. Pratt, nearest her, said:

"Who are you?"

"I'm Miss Rossitter. Mr. Dawlish asked me to come and see him. Unfortunately I was delayed."

Dawlish felt Felicity's gaze, knew that she wanted him to tell Pratt the truth about the woman. He clung stubbornly to the wisdom of seeing Kate on her own, but was concerned now only with Tim and that suffocating hope.

"Take Miss Rossitter into the other room and give her a drink, will you?"

A car turned into the mews. Had the doctor come already? He heard the men clumping up the stairs, and the first to appear was Trivett. With him was a police surgeon from the Yard.

Both men approached the bed while Dawlish slipped away for hot water bottles and electric blanket.

When he returned, the doctor was packing away a hypodermic syringe.

Trivett said, "It's a narcotic, injected into the bloodstream."

The doctor added briskly, "I think he'll do. I'll come back or send someone else in half an hour, to stay here until he starts to come round. That might be in an hour, or sometime tomorrow. With luck, he'll be all right. Ah—hot water bottles, good."

Between them, they pulled up the blankets so that only Tim's pale face showed above them, tucked him in, and then went toward the door.

19
Talk with Kate

Trivett was spruce, alert, eager, as if this were the beginning of the day. Dawlish, feeling the reaction, wanted to sit back without thinking. Trivett allowed him a few minutes to recover, knowing the depth of his friendship with Tim Jeremy.

He said at last, "Who's this Miss Rossitter?"

"A young woman of charm whose activities more than interest me."

"Why?"

"Her father is a good customer of Mr. Jeremiah Kittle."

"The Manchester Rossitter, who does business with Midlon?"

"That's it. How much do you really know about this business, Bill?"

Trivett shrugged. "Not as much as I'd like to. Probably not as much as you do. We still don't know whether Sir Mortimer Kittle was murdered, and if he was, we don't know by whom. We do know that several of his companies were on the verge of bankruptcy, and if he hadn't died, he would soon have been answering some pretty awkward questions."

"I see," said Dawlish, woodenly.

"We also know that some of the businesses were losing money because of the activities of Midlon," Trivett went on. "Did you know all this?"

"I spend my time chasing after will-o'-the-wisps," said Dawlish.

Trivett smiled, knowing better, then went on: "As Kittle's affairs went downhill, Midlon's went up. Midlon has a perfectly respectable board of directors, as far as I can tell. Its business appears to be sound, and if it weren't for the three fires which have interested Safeguard, I doubt if Midlon would have been suspected of anything underhand. Taken at face value, it and the Kittle companies were having cut-throat competition, and Midlon was winning. The Midlon big shot is a man named Dean—Arnold Dean."

Did Trivett know that Dean had a luxury flat under a different name?

"I've met Mr. Dean," said Dawlish.

"They've done a lot of business through Rossitter of Manchester," said Trivett. "Jeremiah Kittle apparently did Rossitter some small service a few years ago, and when he went to see Rossitter, he got some business—on condition that he put it through Midlon. In itself, that isn't surprising —Dean is a shrewd man, and knows the best companies for each kind of insurance, and can force some of the companies to pretty good deals. They specialize in unusual insurances, and one of their specialties is a form of insurance to defeat death duties and, it's rumored, income tax, by taking advantage of legal loopholes. The evidence is that Mortimer Kittle was getting Midlon to find such loopholes for him—and also, the evidence is that he didn't know that Midlon was responsible for a lot of the losses which some of his companies were having. Following?"

"Yes," said Dawlish. He stubbed out his cigarette and lit another. "All very helpful, Bill. To what do I owe this sunny, expansive mood?"

Trivett chuckled.

"It's a job where your nose will probably get more results than our routine. And a job where we can discover nothing criminal. Or there wasn't until you butted in, and stung these people to reprisals. What lies behind it—" he shrugged. "I just don't know. Taken at its face value, it's a case of fierce business competition, in which Midlon managed to get hold of confidential papers from the Kittle companies, used those papers to gain Kittle business, and at the same time, kept friendly with Sir Mortimer, who didn't know who was behind the troubles. The only illegal aspect of that side of the case is the way Kittle twisted and turned to try to keep his companies solvent. That was certainly criminal. I needn't go into details, you can just take my word for it. Of course, this applied only to some of the Kittle companies. Others were good going concerns. It won't prevent Jeremiah Kittle from becoming a millionaire, although it might have earned his cousin a long sentence in jail."

"Meaning?"

"That the first death *could* have been suicide."

Dawlish said, "Hmm, yes. Everyone was presumably satisfied that it wasn't murder, until Sir Mortimer's old mother asked me to look round. She was on the mark in thinking that her son's affairs wouldn't bear close examination, wasn't she?" He laughed shortly. "It was when I started to work on Jeremiah, and Prudence Lorne, that the trouble began. Kemp was the troublemaker. What about the two men at Great Marlborough Street; were they Midlon agents?"

"No. Old lags, ready to turn a hand for any dishonest

100

penny. Kemp used them—by appointment; they didn't know that he lived at that Croydon house, or where they could find him. They knew that he used others—such as the man who shot at Prudence Lorne—"

"Or at me."

"Do you seriously think it was at you?"

"Could have been," said Dawlish.

"It isn't likely. For some reason, Kemp wanted—wants—Prudence Lorne dead. Have you any reason to believe that she's mixed up in it, except by accident?"

"No," said Dawlish.

"How did you find Felicity?"

"I told you—through Kemp."

"What made you think he might be on the train to Manchester?"

"Guesswork—because Jeremiah Kittle had gone up there and been seen in Kemp's company earlier in the day."

Trivett said, "Where is Kemp now?"

"The last I heard, he was at the Midland Hotel, Manchester."

Trivett passed a hand across his face, as if to hide a smile. "Well, you're telling the truth about that," he said. "What is this woman Rossitter doing here?"

"Look, Bill," said Dawlish, "there are things it's better for a good policeman not to know." He tapped the ash from his cigarette, and stretched his legs further out in front of him. "Rossitter might be in the racket, but might also be a businessman with unscrupulous methods who tricked Mortimer Kittle but didn't commit any crime. I think I've got the woman nervous about her father, but that's as far as I can go."

"Nervous?" Trivett's eyebrows shot up. "Is that what you call nervous? Listen, Pat. This case has two distinct sides: Sir Mortimer Kittle's death, the trouble with his companies and the possibility of an insurance racket, makes one. The other is the violence you've stirred up—attacks on Miss Lorne, on Felicity, and now on Tim Jeremy. The two things appear to be connected—and the moment you can uncover a connection, I expect you to tell me."

"I will," said Dawlish.

"Make sure you do," said Trivett sternly.

A few minutes after Trivett had gone off with Pratt, leaving two men on duty outside the mews, Harrison, of Safeguard, arrived.

He was muffled up in a heavy coat and scarf, and although he was as brisk as ever, he seemed to be repressing an unaccustomed excitement.

"Can you spare me a few minutes, Mr. Dawlish?"

As Dawlish led the way into the flat, Harrison said abruptly:

"I want to know why you questioned Renfrew's loyalty."

Dawlish shrugged, "I can't give you chapter and verse, and I may be wrong, but Renfrew isn't all he makes out to be."

Harrison looked at him sharply.

"It's hard to believe. But I have just talked to another of Safeguard's inquiry staff. It's transpired that Renfrew was dealing with Midlon under the assumed name of Anderson. Did you know that?"

"I knew he had an alias."

Harrison said abruptly, "I still find it hard to accept the possibility that he is a rogue. But I give you my full authority to investigate, without consultation with him."

Dawlish smiled faintly. "Thanks."

He saw Harrison off, returned, and stood and listened outside the door of the living room. Kate Rossitter was talking, and it was hard to believe that she was the woman he had held up on the train. She was talking earnestly about the wave of violent crime, the difficulty that the police had in combating it, and she sounded as if she meant every word.

Dawlish opened the door.

". . . it goes deeper than that," Kate was saying. "*Much* deeper. It's the whole moral background of the country; people just aren't so *honest* as they were." She broke off. "Don't you agree, Mr. Dawlish?" She smiled at him with warmth and charm. "It's nice to see you again—and in a milder mood. You quite frightened me on the train."

"And Kemp?"

"I'm afraid he's a weak character," said Kate sorrowfully. "As a matter of fact—" she paused, as if uncertain how her next words would be received. "I feel responsible for him. Do you believe in trying to reform bad characters, Mr. Dawlish?"

Dawlish sat on the arm of a chair.

"Some are beyond redemption," he said.

"Oh, you mustn't think that! I'm sure there's good in Ronnie Kemp. He did tell you where your charming wife could be found. I would have told you if he hadn't, of course, although not then. You see—" she paused again.

Dawlish said lightly, "Nice of you."

"The trouble is that I'm afraid you won't believe me," said Kate Rossitter earnestly. "I acted the part of an unscrupulous adventuress almost too well!" She laughed, musically. "You see, I'm trying to find out who employs Kemp. He, they, are blackmailing my father. The only way I could hope to gain their confidence was to become friendly with Kemp." She looked up at Dawlish, her eyes glowing with honesty. "That's why I was *delighted* that you're taking an interest."

Kate leaned forward, with a gesture both earnest and

eager. "You see, there's so little I can do alone to help my father. Like most victims of blackmail he wasn't always the upright, sober citizen that he is now." She smiled a little ruefully. "That's why I didn't want the police brought in. You can't think how happy and relieved I was when you came on the scene! Then I had a message from a Mr. Dean. I called to see him, and then came straight here. One of the reasons I'm not too happy about him is that he has a flat in Baker Street under the assumed name of Morgan. But if he *is* a villain, he would hardly have sent me to see the very man I want to beg for help, would he?"

20

Somersault

Unable to keep still any longer, Felicity poured out more drinks. Her hand was unsteady. Kate kept her eyes on Dawlish, adoring, beseeching spaniel's eyes. The room was very quiet, and there were no sounds outside. It was hard to believe that Tim lay in the next room hovering between life and death; that this was the woman who had shown the gun in the train. It was harder to believe that she had any hope that Dawlish would believe her. But she appeared to be quite certain that he would.

Kate said, "So I've come to tell you *every*thing."

"Very commendable," said Dawlish dryly.

"You *will* help, won't you?"

Dawlish said solemnly that he would.

"That's wonderful! I know I can take your word for it," Kate assured him enthusiastically. "There's no need, of course, to tell you of my father's past, only that for years he's been paying blackmail to a man who died only a few days ago. I'm talking about Sir Mortimer Kittle—the millionaire. The most hateful man I've ever met. When he died, we thought everything was all over—and then the blackmail started again."

"I see," said Dawlish.

"So someone else must have shared the secret," said Kate. "Kemp knows who it is, but I haven't been able to make Kemp talk freely yet. I think he will—if you'll leave him to me." She looked appealing. "I think my methods would be best with him, don't you?"

"Possibly," said Dawlish woodenly.

"Of course, there's little Jeremiah Kittle," said Kate. "He's so sweet. My father has given him some business, just to help him. He's very sentimental, you know."

"Your father must be a fine character," said Dawlish.

"Oh, Father *is*. He's quite the most wonderful man I know. That's why I'm so desperately anxious that a man like you should help him. There are moments when I feel that I'm not equal to it, and I'm frightened. I carry a gun everywhere, just in case of need. It was lucky I did last night, it was the one thing which finally convinced Kemp that I wanted to help him. The whole mystery turns on the identity of his boss, I think—don't you?"

"It could."

"I feel sure it does. Well, I think I've told you everything, and—oh, but I haven't. I've forgotten Jimmy."

Her expression became earnest again, and carried a hint of fear.

"If I hadn't promised to tell you everything, I wouldn't mention Jimmy," she said. "Jimmy Anderson, I mean. I wonder—" She turned slowly to Felicity, hesitated as if anxious to choose exactly the right words, and then went on: "I wonder if *you* know what I mean, Mrs. Dawlish, when I say that the man has a kind of fatal fascination for me. He's so cold—aloof—inhuman, almost. He *hypnotizes* me. I can't explain what I feel about him, except that there are times when I like him very much, and other times when he repels me. He says so little, yet seems to know almost everything."

106

Dawlish said, "Such as?"

"Well, he knows that my father has been blackmailed. Then there were fires at two of my father's small factories, quite recently. Jimmy was there—"

"At the time of the fire?"

"Well, immediately afterwards, and Ronnie says that he was actually near one of the factories the day before the outbreak. Do you know him?"

"I've never met a man named James Anderson," Dawlish said.

"Well, I think you ought to," said Kate diffidently. "He has a flat in Maybury Court, and a country cottage, too, I believe."

She smoothed out her skirt. "Well, that's everything, I think. I'm afraid I was a little late, but I couldn't find a taxi. That was a terrible sight in the yard. Was that man dead?"

"Nearly."

"What a gruesome thing to do," Kate shuddered. "Who on earth thought of it? A *coffin*. And that flame! If you hadn't been so quick you'd have been blinded!" She broke off, and then began to laugh, the lovely sound filling the room. "But I'm crazy! I've done all the talking, and haven't even asked you why you wanted me to come!"

There was a pause.

"What *did* you want me for?" she asked.

Dawlish said, "To get information about Kemp."

"Well, I've given you that." She yawned delicately. "Is that all?"

"Nearly all," said Dawlish. "I wanted—"

The telephone rang, making Kate look quickly toward it. Had she expected a call?

What should he do? Pretend—although she would know it was pretense—that he believed her? Or cut through the nonsense and get tough?

Felicity said, "Just a minute," and turned from the telephone. "It's Ted, Pat."

Dawlish put the receiver to his ear, while Felicity stood looking at him anxiously.

"How quickly can you get up here?" Ted asked, without preamble.

"Is it as urgent as that?"

"I think so. I can get police protection or I can wait for you." Ted sounded in sober earnest. "They're gunning for me. I had a lucky break, but—"

He broke off.

"But what?" Dawlish's voice was harsh with anxiety.

Ted said, "Sorry, I thought I heard someone at the door. Believe it or not, I'm jittery. Did a crazy thing, and tried to break into Rossitter's house. They spotted me and have been up to their tricks ever since. Shall I wait for you?"

Dawlish said, "No. Tell the police."

"If it will help to wait—"

"Get off the line, and then call them," said Dawlish. "There are limits to folly. I'll come up as soon as I can."

"Good man," said Ted. He sounded relieved. "Love to Felicity—and tell Joan I won't be home for a day or two, will you?"

The line went dead.

21

Dawlish in a Hurry

Dawlish put down the receiver, smiled mechanically at Felicity, said "I'll be back in a minute," and ran quickly downstairs. The night air stung his damp forehead.

Pratt came across the mews.

"Want me, Mr. Dawlish?"

"I certainly do. Telephone Mr. Trivett, and ask him to get in touch with the Manchester police immediately. Mr. Beresford—he'll know who I mean—is having trouble at the Grand Hotel and needs help. Beresford will call your Manchester people, but they may not pay him much attention. Will you fix it?"

"Can I say what kind of trouble?"

"Someone's gunning for Beresford."

"Right." Pratt turned and raced away.

Dawlish went back to the flat, stopping outside Tim's door. He could hear no sound. Farther on, Kate was talking again. He found himself wondering if there could be any truth in what she had said, and although he dismissed the thought impatiently, it harassed him. Was he right to avoid direct action, to let her go, uttering words as fatuous as hers had been?

Supposing he told her he didn't believe a word of what she had told him? Would that come off? Probably not—she was too astute, her mind too quick. If he threatened to consult the police, she would reproach and defy him. Her version of the incident in the sleeping car would be as convincing as his. He tried to imagine Kate in the dock, answering counsel; she would have a jury with her almost from the first word.

The door opened, and Felicity came onto the landing, her voice sharp with anxiety.

"What's the trouble with Ted?"

"SOS. He's rattled."

"If Ted's nervous—"

"Yes, it's bad," Dawlish said. "Question—what to do with the garrulous beauty?"

"Could there be anything in what she says?"

"I thought it impressed you," Dawlish said.

"I couldn't help wondering," Felicity glanced at the door. "She's so young, and so pretty."

"No guarantee of virtue, I fear," Dawlish said dryly. "The question remains—what to do with her. Let her go, or ask the police to follow her?"

"If the police follow, she'll know you don't believe her."

"She can't seriously think I do."

"I think she does," said Felicity. "Pat, why not let me see what I can do with her?"

Dawlish said, "Have you forgotten that where you go, Squire Pratt also goes?"

"I could soon shake him off if I wanted to," said Felicity calmly.

"No shaking off," said Dawlish. He put his arm around her shoulder. "There's been too much emotional strain from the beginning. First you, then Tim—now Ted. The fact is, when you're on the danger list, I'm simply not responsible for what I do. Don't take any more chances, whether I'm around or not."

He looked away, not wanting her to see how shaken he still was, then went on, in a rather muffled voice, "Talking of Ted, they're probably working on him so as to lure me to Manchester. That could be because they don't want me in London."

"Then why go?"

"Fly walking deliberately into the neatly woven web," said Dawlish. "I'll be reasonably happy if I know you're inside these four walls and the Yard is looking after you. And we'll let Kate go her own sweet way. If the police decide to follow her, that won't be our fault. She's keeping very quiet."

Dawlish pushed open the door and stopped on the threshold. Kate Rossitter made a sight worth seeing. She lay back in her chair, youthful and lovely, in an attitude of absolute relaxation. Her eyes were closed.

"She *can't* be asleep," whispered Felicity.

Dawlish went forward noiselessly. The girl didn't stir. He stood staring down at her, then gently touched her right eyelid. He raised it. She didn't move, didn't suggest by the slightest movement that she knew that she was being touched.

"Dope?" Felicity suggested.

Dawlish let the eyelid fall, and then picked up a heavy ashtray and dropped it. It fell with noise enough to waken anyone out of a deep sleep.

"There's a doctor in the other room," Felicity said. "Shall I go and get him?"

Dawlish nodded.

Kate Rossitter was sleeping under the effect of a mild narcotic, the young doctor said. She would probably sleep through the night. He did not think there was the slightest risk of serious consequences.

111

Tim would pull through, too; he'd take a few days to get back to normal, but was in no acute danger.

Pratt came forward as Dawlish, wearing an overcoat and cap, appeared at the front door.

He explained briefly about Kate Rossitter and asked that the two women have an extra guard.

Two minutes later the Bentley was purring out of the mews on the way to Croydon Airport.

An hour and three quarters after leaving the flat, Dawlish was on the Manchester road; in fifteen minutes, his taxi pulled up outside the darkened doors of the Grand Hotel.

Dawlish got out.

"You know you're going to stand by all night, don't you?" he asked the driver.

"Yes, sir, all okay."

Dawlish went into the hotel. Inside, a big man in plain clothes, with "detective" written all over him, was talking to the night porter. He looked up.

"Mr. Dawlish?"

"That's right. Anything happened here?"

"Mr. Beresford is still in his room," said the Manchester detective. "I know he's expecting you. There was some trouble about two hours ago; a man actually shot the lock off the door, but we caught him."

"Nice work." Dawlish moved toward the elevator, in the wake of the night porter.

"Room 55, sir," said the porter. "I'll take you there."

"Have you a master key?" asked Dawlish.

"Yes, sir, but—"

"Let's use it," said Dawlish, "there's no need to wake him."

The lock clicked back and Dawlish opened the door an

inch. There was no further sound, nothing to suggest that Ted was awake.

Dawlish switched on the light, and it blazed about a deserted room and a rumpled, empty bed.

22

Frightened Man

"But he was here!" gasped the porter. "I brought him up some beer myself, I spoke to him!"

Dawlish went quickly to the bed and touched the sheets; they were cold.

"He was in bed," the porter said, still agitatedly. "He said he hoped to make up on the sleep he'd lost last night."

Dawlish crossed to the wardrobe. No clothes hung in it, but Ted's pigskin suitcase was in the bottom, containing a few oddments. His shaving kit was neatly displayed. Dawlish went to the window. It faced a blank wall. There was a sheer drop below, and no fire escape within reach. Ted, with his artificial leg, wouldn't have had a chance.

"He didn't pass through the front hall," the porter said firmly. "If I haven't been there, the detective has."

"Back way," murmured Dawlish. "Shall we have a look at the fire escape?"

The door leading to the escape was unlocked. Some time after sending for that beer, Ted had dressed, taken his automatic, and gone out. Dawlish went back to the room, and sent the porter down to report to the detective. Then he opened the suitcase again, unfolded some handkerchiefs, and examined a pair of socks, shaking each in turn. A slip of paper fell from the second.

Dawlish took it to the light, and read Ted's almost indecipherable writing:

Fooled 'em, I think; they're sure I'm scared stiff. They were listening in to that talk we had. Sorry if I alarmed you! I'm going to see Kemp, then on to R's place.

Dawlish chuckled aloud, slipped the note into his pocket, and went downstairs.

The Manchester detective was at the telephone on the porter's desk, talking rapidly.

"I'll take over from Mr. Beresford," Dawlish said to the porter. "Put my bag in his room, will you?" Without waiting for an answer, he hurried into the dark night, and turned to the waiting car. "The Midland Hotel," he directed briefly.

In five minutes, his driver pulled up outside the Midland. The one porter on duty came forward briskly.

"Have you a room, sir?"

"Oh, yes," said Dawlish, and stifled a gargantuan yawn. "What are the chances of a cup of tea and a sandwich?"

"Well, sir—"

"Be a hero," Dawlish said. "I'll have them down here, I want to make a telephone call." Silver changed hands and the porter went off. Dawlish made a dive to the reception desk. He opened the register, ran his forefinger down the previous day's entries, and found Miss Kathleen Rossitter and Mr. Ronald Kemp; Kemp's room was 37.

So neither of them had tried to hide their names.

Dawlish was faintly amused and encouraged by Ted's trick. Ted wouldn't have come here and then gone to Ribbleton Street if he weren't sure that the night sortie held prospects. Dawlish went up the stairs, reached the third floor without encountering anyone, and turned toward the right.

A faint rustle of sound stopped him.

His hand dropped to his gun as he drew his head back and waited.

Then he heard the sound again; a footfall, soft and stealthy. A man was peering around the far corner.

Dawlish lay down at full length, then risked another peep. The man was now only three yards away, and held a gun. As a foot came into sight, Dawlish launched himself forward, left hand outstretched. He gripped an ankle and tugged. The gun went off with a muted sound as the man toppled over. Dawlish smashed his left fist into the other's jaw. The head jolted back, then hit the floor with a thud loud enough to wake people in the nearer bedrooms.

The gun and silencer fell to the carpet. Dawlish pocketed it, then stepped to the nearest door. It opened at a touch, revealing a chambermaid's pantry. He went back, hauled the man's inert body through the door, then tore a tea towel into strips and bound the man's wrists and ankles.

Behind the door hung a bunch of keys. He took them and went out, walking quickly along the passage to Room 37.

Gently he turned the handle. The door was locked. He tried two of the keys without success, but the third turned with a faint click. Dawlish waited, but heard no stirring inside the room. He opened the door and saw darkness beyond. As he slipped inside, he heard the ticking of a clock but no sound of a man breathing. The narrow beam of his torch touched the end of a bed. Cautiously Dawlish moved the light along its length.

It shone on a glistening red patch.

The light quivered, then steadied. Dawlish stared at the patch, and knew that it was blood. He let the light travel

116

upwards again, and it shone upon another, larger patch of red, on a throat which had been slashed—and on the face of Ronnie Kemp.

Dawlish switched on the light, scanning each corner of the large, well-furnished room. It was obvious that it had been searched. He opened the wardrobe, then tried the door leading to the next room; it was locked from the other side. He pushed a heavy armchair toward it, to avoid being surprised, then turned to the bed. His own face was set; violent death is a shocking thing, no matter who the victim.

Dawlish touched Kemp's hand; it was warm with natural warmth. The glistening crimson of the blood was fresh.

Dawlish hurried downstairs, in time to stop the porter from entering the elevator.

"Sorry," he said. "I had to have a wash."

"Tea'll be stewed," the porter said aggrievedly.

"Never mind," said Dawlish. He poured himself out a cup. "I'm not so hungry as I thought; maybe I'll feel like these upstairs." He gulped the tea down, took the plate of sandwiches and went upstairs again, the porter tagging behind. If the man insisted on entering the room, trouble would come too quickly.

The porter left him at the third floor landing. Dawlish put the sandwiches on the floor, went for the prisoner, and carried him to Kemp's room.

Dawlish sat the man in an armchair, facing Kemp. He switched on the light over the head of the bed; it made the ugly wound look even ghastlier. Watching his victim closely, he noted the first flickering of the nerves, the mutter of returning consciousness. The man's eyes opened, closed, then sprang wide.

Transfixed, they stared at Kemp.

117

It was impossible to tell whether he had seen Kemp like this before or not. Slowly, his gaze swiveled around, and came to Dawlish.

Dawlish said, "Why did you kill him?"

The man didn't answer, but fear showed in his eyes.

Dawlish looked through the papers which he'd taken from the prisoner's wallet. There were several cards bearing the name Midlon Insurance Brokers and one printed: *"Mr. K. J. Morris."*

"Do I have to knock the answer out of you?" Dawlish asked.

Fear deepened in the gray eyes. Dawlish moved toward him, towering, his face set, his hands clenched—but the man didn't speak.

Dawlish said, "Who told you to kill him?"

There was still no answer, but the man's lips worked. Dawlish heard a sound, from the door.

Someone was turning the handle.

23

Fear

Dawlish moved away from the man in the chair. A single cry from Morris would warn whoever was outside, but he took the chance. The handle was turning slowly. He reached the door and unlocked it. As the final click came, he pulled the door open and shot out his free hand.

He was a split second too late.

A man with a scarf around the lower part of his face and a hat pulled low down over his forehead backed swiftly away, turned on his heel, and ran. Dawlish lunged forward, dislodging the hat.

He saw that the man was Renfrew. By the time he reached the corner, he was out of sight. Dawlish turned back. He could think about Renfrew later.

The other man sat helplessly in the chair, his forehead beaded with sweat.

He said faintly, "I didn't kill Kemp. I worked with him. He sent me along to see if anyone was coming. He was alive when I left him."

"Why did he send you out of the room?"

"He thought he heard the lift. He was nervous—he expected to be attacked. He thought it would be you." The man licked his lips, then muttered, "I believe *you* killed him."

Dawlish said calmly, "You worked with Kemp at the Midlon, did you?"

"Yes, I did!"

"Who else did he work for?"

"Rossitter. He gave the orders."

"Do you know Miss Rossitter?"

"Know her?" The man's lips twisted. "I hate the sight of her! So did Kemp. He was terrified of her. She isn't a woman, she's a fiend!"

"Why was Kemp staying here?"

"She told him to. She told me to wait with him and keep an eye on him."

"What else do you know?"

The man's tongue darted along his dry lips.

"I don't know what you're after. Kemp fixed a high insurance on broken-down factories, I—"

"You fired them, did you?"

The man muttered, "I had to. If I hadn't, they would have given me hell."

"Told anyone else about this?"

"No, no, I—" the man broke off. "You're Dawlish, aren't you? I don't know who frightened Kemp most, you or that woman. I know who frightens *me*. Dawlish, be a sport, send for the police."

He sounded as if he meant it.

"Send for them," the prisoner pleaded. "Until I'm charged, I shan't feel safe. The man who killed Kemp will have a go at me. Man or woman, that bi—"

"Kate's in London, so she couldn't have killed Kemp."

"She could have fixed it. She was afraid he was going to talk. That's why I had to watch him—to stop him from giving anything away. But I can't stand any more. I'll tell the police everything I know."

Dawlish said, "Maybe I'll send for the police. Or I could telephone Kate, and tell her the mood you're in."

The man gasped: "No!"

"How many factories did you burn?"

"Three!"

"Have you come across a man named Renfrew?"

"Ren-frew? No, I don't remember the name."

"Anderson?"

"Oh, I know Anderson," said the prisoner, glad that he was able to say so. "He did some business with Kemp. Cold-blooded devil, he gives me the creeps."

Dawlish said, "What did Kemp and Anderson work on?"

"I don't know. Anderson worked with one of the big insurance companies. Kemp handled a lot of Midlon's work. I was on the payroll, but I just did what Kemp told me, and he made me set fire to those factories. It was the woman who fixed it; he just carried out her orders, using any stooge he could find."

"Including Anderson?"

"I wouldn't know."

Dawlish said, "Did anyone else come to see Kemp to-night?"

"Yes, a big man forced his way in and tried to make Kemp talk. I was hiding in the wardrobe. Kemp didn't give anything away. We thought he might be from Kate, just testing us out."

So Ted Beresford had tried here, and failed; there was some evidence that Morris was telling the truth. Dawlish watched him, trying to make sure whether anything was being kept back. The man seemed genuinely terrified. It looked as if he really meant that he would rather be in the hands of the police than free and at Kate's mercy.

"What's Rossitter like to look at?"

"He's just ordinary, on the small side. Dawlish, I can't tell you anything more—"

"Is he a partner in Midlon?"

"He is Midlon. Even Dean's scared of Rossitter and his daughter. Dean's bad enough, but the Rossitters—"

"So Dean knows about the fire racket?"

"Of course he knows!"

Dawlish said, "Think it over for half an hour. I'll come back and see if you've remembered anything else. Then I'll consider calling the police."

"Dawlish!" Morris's cry was urgent. "Don't leave me alone, anything might happen. I'm scared, I just haven't got what it takes. Send for the police and stay with me until they come."

Dawlish said, "Courage, little man."

He went out, but he was not happy. Morris's fear had been contagious; Dawlish was prepared to believe that whoever had killed Kemp would attack the other. He slipped into the chambermaid's pantry and took the telephone receiver off the hook.

He said tersely, "Please connect me with the police."

"Police?"

"There's been some trouble on the third floor, Room 37. It's urgent."

"Who—"

"Never mind who I am, give me the police!"

The man muttered, "I can't put you through, but I'll call them. Room 37 did you say? What—what kind of trouble?"

"Murder." Dawlish put the receiver down sharply, and stepped into the passage. He stood outside the door of 37 but heard nothing. He waited for seven minutes, by his watch, then heard the whine of the elevator. He slipped back to the pantry, leaving the door ajar. The elevator stopped, and three men, including a constable in uniform, walked stolidly toward Number 37. Dawlish waited until he heard Morris cry out, first in fear, then in relief.

In the hall, the porter was talking earnestly to two constables. He caught sight of Dawlish, and broke off, pointing wildly:

"That's the man!"

"That's right," said Dawlish. "I telephoned you. My name is Dawlish."

The two constables approached warily.

"Mr. Patrick Dawlish?"

"Certainly. There was a request from Scotland Yard for you people to give me help if I needed it." He wasn't sure whether the news had penetrated as far down the ranks as these men but went on steadily: "Have Mr. Trivett of Scotland Yard informed about what happened upstairs, and ask him to make sure that Miss Rossitter is still at my flat."

"Anything else, sir?"

"No, thanks." Dawlish nodded authoritatively and went out. The chauffeur of his hired car was walking briskly up and down, beating his arms across his chest. He sprang to the door as Dawlish approached.

"Where to now, sir?"

"Salford way," said Dawlish. "Ribbleton Street."

A yellow fog hung gloomily over the trams and streetlights. Thoughts crowded into Dawlish's mind, most of them anxious. Kate had lied, not the little man now being questioned by the police. Kate had lied—and she was in the flat with Felicity. Would Pratt be able to prevent her from doing any harm? Would she risk an open attack, now? He didn't think so, but the possibility remained like a nagging toothache. Why had she taken that drug? Had it been administered without her realizing it, or had she drugged herself so that she could stay at the flat?

"Fog's getting worse," muttered the chauffeur. He inched

around two corners, then pulled up with a flourish. "Better have a look first. Won't be a jiff."

As he moved away, a big, shadowy figure appeared on the opposite pavement. Dawlish dropped his right hand to his pocket. But there was no need for his gun; it was Ted Beresford.

24

Rossitter's House

Dawlish opened the door, and Ted climbed in, dropping heavily onto the seat.

"So you got my note?"

"Nicely done," murmured Dawlish.

"It's about all that has gone well," growled Ted. "I tried to frighten Kemp out of his wits, but it was no go."

"You don't have to try any more," Dawlish said.

Ted looked at him sharply and comprehendingly: "I'm not really surprised—poor little devil." His fingers, as he took a cigarette from Dawlish, were ice cold. "I thought I could break into any jail, but Rossitter's house beat me. It would have done Hitler proud."

"Any prowlers about?" asked Dawlish.

"One caller, turned up about an hour ago."

"Who was it?"

"Male, sprightly, youngish, I should say."

"Who let him in?"

"A man—I couldn't see, but I could hear. I also heard the chains going up at the door, and the bolts shooting home," Ted said. "Waste of an evening." He was gloomy.

"Perhaps Rossitter will give us breakfast."

"How will you get in? Knock at the door and ask to see him?" Ted asked derisively.

"Yes," said Dawlish.

Before Ted could comment, the chauffeur came back.

"We're going to pay a call along here," Dawlish said, smiling at the man's astonishment at finding two passengers instead of one. "I want you to stay somewhere handy so that when we come out we can move off in a hurry. Is there a side turning off Ribbleton Street?"

"Three."

"Take the one in the middle."

The chauffeur let in the clutch and they moved off, pulling up about ten yards along the side street.

Ted got out and Dawlish followed him. They strolled along toward the main road end together. Ted said: "An accommodating chap. Who is he?"

"Officially, a Manchester taxi driver, though it wouldn't surprise me to know he's on the Manchester C.I.D. plainclothes staff. The police wouldn't really give me such a free hand as they seem to be doing without some pretty strong motive."

"Meaning?"

Dawlish chuckled softly.

"I think the force has been waiting to get a crack at Rossitter and Midlon for a long time. Until now, they haven't had a chance to do anything officially. When I happened along, Trivett decided that I would probably bludgeon a way through. On that bright hope he is willing to wink at irregularities—but is determined to find out what's really happening."

Ted stopped outside Number 81. It had, Dawlish noted, a seven-foot walled garden, and stood too far back from the road to be visible. There were tall iron gates in the middle of the wall, and a wide driveway.

"Funny," said Ted.

"What is?"

"Those gates were open when I last came here."

Dawlish tried the big iron handle, but the gates were locked. Ted shrugged and linked his hands in an impromptu stepping block. Dawlish grasped one of the bars of the gate, stepped onto Ted's hands, then onto his shoulders. Ted stood massive and unmoving as Dawlish leapt, landing on all fours.

He straightened up, brushing the gravel from his gloves and knees, then took out his knife, and in the dim light of the streetlamp began to work on the padlock. It was a simple one; no special precautions had been taken here.

He unfastened the padlock calmly.

"Open sesame," he said, and opened one of the gates.

They walked along the wide graveled drive, making no particular attempt to conceal themselves. The house loomed suddenly through the muffling mist, lights at two windows.

Dawlish pressed the bell. No one answered.

There was a large iron knocker. Ted wielded it vigorously, then each man stood facing the door, his right hand in his pocket.

A moment later there was a sound, as of someone pulling a chain out of its running socket. The big men stood like statues, not a muscle of their faces moving, with their guns clenched tightly.

A man opened the door, and said in a dispassionate voice:

"I suppose that's you, Dawlish."

It was Renfrew.

Renfrew moved ahead of them in the large, square hall, then turned with his back to the staircase.

Dawlish said amiably: "Hello. Whose throat are you going to cut next?"

"It depends who gets in my way." Renfrew's smile was

derisive. "And you?—haven't you finished blundering about yet?"

"I'm still looking for a murderer."

"I'm not sure that Sir Mortimer Kittle *was* murdered," said Renfrew. "I am sure that Midlon is corrupt from top to bottom. I was going to have another go at Kemp tonight, but you stopped me. I came on here. I've found sufficient papers to prove that the fires at the factories were arson. I can put Dean, Kemp, and everyone connected with Midlon on the spot—except Rossitter."

Dawlish said generously, "For a man who doesn't talk much, you're doing well."

"There's a time to talk and a time to keep your mouth shut. You wouldn't know anything about the latter." The voice was cold and sardonic, but there was no doubt that Renfrew was both handsome and striking. "I've nearly finished my job. I don't even care much whether I get anything on Rossitter or not; the police can probably rope him in."

Dawlish, watching him, calculated that if Renfrew had a weakness, it was overconfidence.

"When you've a minute to spare," Dawlish said pleasantly, "you might tell me how you managed to get into Rossitter's house, dig out this information, and stay long enough to let in stray callers."

"Use your imagination. If you wanted to get information about a certain householder, what would be the best way to set about it? I'll tell you. Bribe one of the household staff. When the boss is away, get him to let you have the freedom of the house. This boss is away, and so is his charming daughter. The only occupant of the house is the man I've bribed—and he's the only servant who lives in; the others come by day. It cost me a hundred pounds, and it was worth it. I told him to go to bed and to hear nothing. He

128

won't show up until half past seven. Until then, I can do what I like."

"You're quite a boy, aren't you, Anderson?" Dawlish murmured.

Renfrew laughed.

"Anderson, Renfrew, or Mr. Smith—what does it matter? I called myself Anderson to Kate Rossitter because she might have heard of Renfrew. I called myself Anderson to Prudence Lorne because her uncle might have mentioned my real name when he was at Midlon's offices. I called myself Anderson to Kemp, and made him think I was willing to work any swindle on Safeguard, and he fell for it. Dean and Kate Rossitter also fell—he told them that he had a stooge at Safeguard's, and they arranged to see me here—tomorrow night. That's how I found out about them and where they live. Want to know anything else?"

"The man with the answer for everything," said Dawlish lightly. "Why did you work on Prudence Lorne?"

"Because her uncle worked with Midlon and I thought that might give me a line—I worked on Kate because she is Rossitter's daughter, and I knew Rossitter had dealings with Midlon and Dean. Satisfied?"

"No."

Renfrew laughed. "I don't suppose you will be. I'll tell you this, Dawlish, you've helped me more than you'll ever guess. If these people hadn't been so worried about you, they wouldn't have let me get away with so much. While you keep 'em busy, I take them in the flank. You can't say I didn't give you the opportunity of working with me."

Dawlish said, "Where's this evidence you say you've found?"

"In the strong room." Renfrew turned, and walked along the passage by the stairs. "Care to go down and check what I've told you?"

"Thanks. Lead the way."

Renfrew stepped through a sliding door. A light beyond shone on a flight of stone steps. Dawlish followed him, then stepped back, sliding the door to.

He heard Renfrew shout and thump on the door as he turned the key in the lock.

"Now we'll have a look around," Dawlish said, and dropped the door key into his pocket.

25

Poor Jeremiah

The lofty downstairs rooms at the front of the house were deserted.

Dawlish led the way up the imposing staircase. There were six bedrooms, a dressing room, and a small library which was filled with books in great mahogany bookcases which looked as if they hadn't been opened for years.

"Renfrew knew what he was talking about," Ted remarked.

"He could even have been honest," said Dawlish. "But if he's right and no one's here, when did Jeremiah Kittle leave?"

"Yesterday afternoon or last night," said Ted.

"Could be." Dawlish led the way to the foot of the next flight of stairs. Five doors led off the top landing. Dawlish took one at a time. The first three were empty.

As they approached the fourth door, Ted whispered:

"Renfrew said only one servant was here, didn't he?"

"Yes," Dawlish tried the handle of a door and found it locked. "Try the next."

This door opened, and the light from the landing shone onto a narrow bed, and on the half-covered head of a sleeping man.

Ted whispered, "The half I can see looks as if it would cheerfully kill its grandmother for a fiver."

Dawlish took the key out of the lock, and relocked the door from the landing. "That leaves one more room." He stepped toward it, but before touching the handle, listened at the top of the stairs. He could hear a faint thudding noise. "Stay here, Ted." He hurried downstairs, and as he drew nearer the ground floor, the thudding became louder.

He tapped sharply at the door to the strong room. The thudding stopped immediately.

"Dawlish!" Renfrew must be shouting, but his voice came faintly. "Let me out of here."

"Ten minutes," called Dawlish. He sped back up the two flights of stairs.

"Is he getting impatient?"

"Very. The door will hold out." Dawlish took out his penknife and approached the one locked door on this landing. Metal scraped on metal as the lock sprang back.

The room beyond was in darkness, but that was no guarantee of safety. They stood poised, hearing the sound of breathing. Dawlish felt for the switch, pressed it down, and flung the door back.

An old man cried out from the single bed. He had been asleep, and this had jolted him awake and left him with arms outstretched, hair sticking up at the back of his head, face working. He needed a shave, and looked as if he hadn't washed for days.

This was Jeremiah Kittle.

Dawlish and Beresford moved forward, and the man's lips began to quiver. Terror flamed in his eyes as he reared back against the wall.

Dawlish stopped abruptly. "It's all right," he said, and there was much gentleness in his voice. "It's all right, we've come to help."

Jeremiah Kittle didn't speak.

132

"We're alone in the house," Dawlish went on. "The others aren't here."

Jeremiah cried out: "Rossitter! Rossitter!"

"No, he's not here, don't worry."

"Rossitter," sighed Jeremiah, but he seemed to have understood, and relaxed a little. Dawlish took out his flask; would whiskey be too strong for the old man in his present state?

Ted said, "I'll get some water."

"Water," croaked Jeremiah. "I've had nothing—nothing to eat or drink. They—they're torturing me!"

"They won't hurt you again," Dawlish said. "We'll have you out of here before Rossitter comes back."

Ted came in with a glass of water, and the old man clutched it with trembling hands.

"I—I've almost forgotten. What day is it?"

The note in the croaking voice was pitiable; it was hard to realize this was the self-important little man into whom Dawlish had cannoned in Green Street only two days ago.

"Friday," Dawlish said. "You came here on Wednesday evening—just two days ago."

Jeremiah closed his eyes.

"I can't understand it," he muttered. "He—he was my friend, my best friend, I can't believe that he would do this to me. He wanted—"

Ted said eagerly, "What did he want?"

"Want?" echoed Jeremiah. "Oh, yes—yes." He shuddered violently. "They wanted me—to make over—my share in—the companies. They wanted me to sign away my fortune. They threatened my wife. Is she all right?"

"Yes, she's fine," said Dawlish. "And—"

"Pru?"

"You needn't worry about either of them, they're being looked after."

Jeremiah said, "Thank God." He leaned back on his pillows and closed his eyes. "If it hadn't been for—"

He broke off, then started again.

"The girl," said Jeremiah. "She—promised—to help. She—tried—to—give—me—a—drink. A—*lovely* girl."

"Rossitter's daughter?" Ted asked.

"Yes, Kate."

Dawlish said easily, "We'll have you out of the place in half an hour. Don't try to talk, there's plenty of time."

Jeremiah shivered.

"Help him to dress, will you, Ted?" Dawlish sounded as if he were already thinking of something else. "I'll go and find out if Renfrew knows anything about this." He stressed the name Renfrew, but Jeremiah took no notice. "Then I'll have a word with Anderson—"

Jeremiah started up.

"Anderson! That brute! Don't trust him, don't trust him! He made me come, made me do what Kemp told me to do. Kemp! Watch Kemp, he—"

"Kemp won't do you any harm," Dawlish said. "What's this about Anderson?"

"He's a friend of Rossitter! Between them they tried to make me sign those papers. Anderson! He held a knife in his hand, he threatened me! If it hadn't been for Kate. He—"

The old man stopped and, although his mouth worked, words wouldn't come. Dawlish turned away. Ted came limping after him, and took his arm.

"Ought we to move him?"

"I think so, Ted."

"Might be wise to have a doctor first. They've nearly driven him off his rocker."

"I think we ought to get out of this place pretty fast."

"Or fetch the police."

"Not yet," said Dawlish. "We aren't quite home yet."

134

Downstairs Renfrew was no longer hammering to be let out. Dawlish slipped the key in the lock and pushed the door open.

As it swung back, Renfrew strode out, wrath in every line.

"You crazy fool! What do you think you're doing?"

"I've been talking to a frightened man," said Dawlish promptly. "Jeremiah Kittle. Odd that you forgot to tell me he was here, isn't it?"

Renfrew said, "Kittle? *Here?*"

"How innocence becomes you!"

Renfrew said, "I don't know what the hell you're talking about. I've got to get out of here, with the dope I've found in that strong room. I thought you were going to play ball, not fool about."

"Odd how different our ideas are," murmured Dawlish.

"The difference lies in the fact that you think you're clever," Renfrew said abruptly, "and I don't. What's this about Kittle being upstairs?"

"Not bad," said Dawlish. "You almost convince me that you didn't know."

He broke off abruptly at a sharp sound at the front door.

Renfrew struck at him with sudden speed, missed, and rushed through the doorway at the end of the passage.

Dawlish let him go. He could get Renfrew whenever necessary, but the opportunity of greeting the callers wouldn't come again. He held his gun inside his pocket, prepared to shoot on sight.

The front door opened slowly, as if it were heavy and the newcomer hadn't the strength to push it hard. Strength—or courage? It opened further, and a small gloved hand showed at one side.

A woman: Prudence or Kate?

Felicity's face appeared around the door.

135

26

Arrival of Kate

Dawlish felt his tension easing, and found himself grinning. Felicity came further, and caught sight of him.

"Pat, you ass!"

"If you could see yourself—"

"It's no time for being funny," said Felicity. "Has she arrived?"

"Who?"

"Kate Rossitter?"

Dawlish said, "Not to my knowledge, sweetheart. What makes you think she might be here?"

"She started out," said Felicity. "We lost her the other side of Manchester."

"Ah," said Dawlish, "it's a big place." He put his arm around Felicity's shoulders, and looked down at her. "Supposing we have it in words of three letters, beginning with why the blazes you've taken a chance and come up here."

"It was that or nothing," Felicity said. "I wouldn't like to do that drive every night of my life, either. Prudence—"

Dawlish said, "For heaven's sake, Felicity! Where does Prudence come in?"

"Here," said Felicity promptly. "She's at the gate. I'll fetch her."

Dawlish stood at the door, watching Felicity disappear into the pale gray mist. He lit a cigarette mechanically, glad of a few minutes to adjust himself to the new development. Questions about the police, who'd let Felicity come, vied in his mind with questions about Renfrew. Waiting until the two women loomed out of the fog, he didn't try to imagine what had happened in London.

"So here we are," said Felicity, nervously. She wasn't sure how Dawlish would react to her arrival, was trying to conceal her uncertainty. "Do you think we could encroach on the hospitality of our unknown host to the point of a cup of tea?"

Dawlish closed the front door and surveyed them. "We'll go into the kitchen and see what we can find, while you make your confession."

"It's partly my fault—" Prudence began.

"We'll apportion the blame later," Dawlish said dryly.

They went along the wide passage to the kitchen. In two minutes, Felicity had filled a kettle, while Prudence was rummaging in a cupboard for the tea caddy.

Felicity said in a small voice, "Pat, I simply had to come. There wasn't even time to telephone—I didn't know the number, anyhow, and wasn't sure you'd be here. Kate came round soon after you'd left. Someone telephoned her. I don't know how she managed it, but she locked Pratt in the bathroom and got out of the flat. She didn't know I'd taken the keys out of her bag while she was asleep. She went out, and was driven off by someone who was waiting for her. I was hurrying after her when Prudence arrived. I remembered you saying that Kate had visited Dean, at the place near Baker Street, and so I thought she might have gone there. As Tim's garage was near, I borrowed his car and we waited outside the flats. Ten minutes later, Kate came out—"

137

"By herself?"

"No, with Dean—he is the fat man, isn't he? They started off at once, and we followed. How could I know that it would be an all-night drive?"

"How indeed," murmured Dawlish.

"Once we were out of London, I had a pretty good idea that they were heading for Manchester. Everything was going all right until we reached Stockport, then the fog—well, it looks as if we got here first," she added.

"It wouldn't surprise me," agreed Dawlish. "And what brought Pru to see you?"

Prudence turned quickly.

"I just couldn't rest," she said. "I wanted to see whether you could give me any more news, and then your wife suggested that I should come with her, and—here I am."

Felicity said, "Pat, it seemed to me that Kate had come to the flat to find out what you were going to do, and when she realized you were going to Manchester, she put on that act, just to fool you. As soon as you were safely out of the way, she—"

"Let's take that for granted," said Dawlish. "Why didn't she deal with you as well as with poor Pratt?"

"I pretended to be asleep," said Felicity, blandly. "That was after I'd gone through her handbag and taken the keys. I didn't know what she was going to do, of course. Actually she locked me in; she didn't realize that thanks to my burglarious husband, I have a master key. It was all cleverly arranged, Pat, and the man who met her must have dealt with the police outside."

"Did anyone come with Kate and Dean?"

"No," said Felicity. "I'm not quite such a fool as I look—"

Dawlish lifted her from her feet in a bearlike hug.

"You're crazy, but I still love you. As for you, Pru, are you sure you turned up just because you couldn't rest?"

"Well—"

Dawlish said crisply, "Truth, please."

Prudence looked worried, and a little evasive. "I had a telephone call from Mortimer Kittle's mother. She said things—horrible things—about Uncle Jerry—" she broke off, with a strangled laugh. "I almost found myself wondering if he could have killed his cousin! Aunt May went to bed early and was asleep, so—well, I came. Have you found Jerry?"

Dawlish said slowly, "Yes, I have."

Her eyes blazed. "Is he all right? Is he—"

"Why shouldn't he be?"

"I just had a feeling that he wouldn't have come up here if he could have helped himself. *Is he all right?*"

"He seems frightened, but otherwise there's nothing the matter with him."

"I must see him," said Prudence urgently.

"Drink your tea, and I'll see what I can do about that later," said Dawlish. He gave her shoulder a reassuring pat, poured out two cups of tea, and carried the tray into the hall. Ted was sitting at the foot of the stairs, looking tired and dejected; he brightened at the sight of the teapot.

"Place is like a morgue," he complained.

"It might be more like one later," said Dawlish, sipping his tea.

"I'm too tired to follow your obscure remarks," said Ted, eating steadily. "Treat me as you would a child."

"That'll come naturally. Kate and the fat boyfriend are around. They must have wanted us to come here, and once they knew I was on the way, followed pretty fast. They're trying to force a climax, and probably wanted us to find what we did find. I don't know whether Renfrew was in their calculations—I doubt it."

Ted said, "Clear as mud."

"It's as clear to you as it is to me," said Dawlish. "I—"

The sound of a shot came sharp and loud. There was a shout, another shot, and as Dawlish reached the door, a scream.

27

Final Killing?

Dawlish reached the door, gun in hand. The scream came again—and then there was a thud. The sound of footsteps came wildly. As they drew nearer, Dawlish could hear a woman's panting breath and the rustle of her clothes. Kate Rossitter, made even lovelier by the fear which shone in her eyes and seemed to glow in her cheeks, rushed out of the strong room and into the hall.

Ted loomed in from in front of her.

"No!" she screamed, and darted to one side. He shot out a long arm, and caught her wrist. She struck at his chest and face, but he held her at arm's length. Gradually she quieted, leaning brokenly against the wall.

Dawlish said, "How did you get in?"

"There's a secret entrance to the strong room," she muttered, "Dean took me that way." She began to shiver. "He's dead." The words sounded like the crack of doom. "He's dead."

"Who's dead?"

"My—father." She swayed, closing her eyes. "Jimmy—Anderson—killed him."

Dawlish said, "How do you know it was Jimmy?"

"He was downstairs, he—" she broke off.

Dawlish said, "Take her to the kitchen, Ted, and tell Felicity to watch her. If she hasn't a gun, give her yours, will you? I'll go and find out what's on downstairs."

"Right." Ted put his arm around Kate, and led her, half fainting, toward the kitchen.

There was still no sound downstairs; the sudden eruption of shooting and running had faded as if it had never happened.

No one was in sight. Gun in hand, Dawlish went down the stone steps, keeping close to the near side wall. Reaching the bottom, he saw that there was a lighted room beyond, the door of which stood open. Two or three big safes were in sight—and, just visible, the legs of a man on the floor. Dawlish drew nearer, and heard a sound that might have been a sharp intake of breath.

Dawlish could see, now, that the man on the floor was Renfrew, and that another man was sitting on a packing case clutching his leg. It was Dean. There was blood on his hands, and blood had trickled from his leg to the floor. By his foot was an automatic pistol. Beyond him, a third man lay in a crumpled heap, his gray hair ruffled, his back to Dawlish; like Renfrew, he was absolutely still.

Dawlish said mildly, "Well, well."

Dean started violently, and grabbed at the gun by his foot. Dawlish kicked it away, then moved across to the farther door, closed it, and turned the key.

"I feel safer that way," he said. "I hope you don't mind."

Dean gasped, "Renfrew shot Rossitter. I was too late to stop him. Renfrew shot me, too, but I got him—the devil! I got Renfrew."

Dawlish could see the wound in Renfrew's head. He could see, too, that the gray-haired man had been shot above the eyes; death must have been instantaneous. Going nearer, he saw that it was Harrison of Safeguard.

"Is Kate all right?" muttered Dean.

"It depends what you mean by all right."

"Look after her," begged Dean. "She's had a rough time. She had an urgent message from her father; he was afraid there was going to be trouble up here. She came to help."

Dawlish said, "Really!"

"I mean it. You'll never know what sacrifices that girl's made for her father. She's been afraid for a long time that he was crooked. All her energy and courage have been spent trying to save his victims without betraying him; but it was a waste of time. A waste of time."

"And you helped her," Dawlish said.

"Someone had to. It's very simple, Dawlish. Midlon, a thoroughly sound organization, was being used for insurance and company rackets. Harrison, or Rossitter, was responsible. Under that name, he was the agent for the north and the Midlands. I thought he was just trying to drive Sir Mortimer Kittle out of business, but it was more than that. He had planned a series of false insurance claims, drove Kittle to commit suicide, and then started to work on Jeremiah Kittle." Dean's head jerked up. "Is Jeremiah all right?"

"Yes."

"I'm glad about that," said Dean. "At least he'll live to forget it, and not be harassed. I wonder if you could help me upstairs, Dawlish, and then send for a doctor."

"Soon," said Dawlish.

He went across to Renfrew. He didn't speak as he felt Renfrew's pulse, didn't glance up at Dean, but sensed the tension in the man. He let Renfrew's hand fall, heavily, and stood up. "I'll help you upstairs." He helped Dean to his feet. Halfway up the stairs, Dawlish heard footsteps and voices. When he reached the passage, his chauffeur appeared, with two other men.

"Everything all right?" the chauffeur asked sharply.

"Not quite," said Dawlish. "Police?"

"Yes, sir, I had—"

"Don't apologize. I thought the police had turned you into a cabby for the occasion," said Dawlish. "Mr. Dean wants a doctor, and then will give a statement. There are two dead men downstairs."

He left Dean to the police, and turned and hurried back to Renfrew. He didn't need to feel the pulse to know that he was alive. Renfrew might be unconscious for hours, even days, but he'd pull out of it.

The chauffeur appeared.

"By gum, you meant it!" He stood in the doorway, as if hypnotized by the two inert bodies.

"I half meant it," said Dawlish. "Will you—"

Behind the chauffeur loomed Trivett. His gaze traveled over the strong room.

"So they were in it together," he said.

"Up to their necks," said Dawlish. "But Dean labors under one misapprehension. Renfrew, alias Anderson, is alive."

Trivett snapped, "Is he, then!"

More men came in, and Renfrew was carried by two of them up the stairs and out to an ambulance.

Dawlish walked slowly upstairs. Trivett was waiting by the front door. His voice, as he turned to Dawlish, was more than satisfied. It was happy.

"We knew there was a lot of funny business in this job, but cracking open a man in Harrison's position was next door to impossible for the police. So I used you. Sorry—but thanks."

"Tell me what you think it was all about."

"Simple," said Trivett. "We've got it all sewn up, thanks to Morris—the prisoner you left for us at the Midland Hotel—and other odds and ends of information. Midlon was being used by one partner, Rossitter—alias Harrison apparently—to work the insurance racket and to smash Sir Mortimer Kittle. Rossitter and Kittle were once friends, as I knew, and obviously fell out. There was vicious enmity between them. The Safeguard directors were worried by the insurance, half suspected that their man Renfrew was corruptible, and didn't begin to suspect Harrison. Renfrew, no doubt, blackmailed Harrison. Finally, he killed him— the one man who could swear that he had turned crooked."

"Ah," said Dawlish dryly. "And you believe all this?"

Trivett looked at him sharply, then went on: "Before that, Renfrew killed Kemp, who could also give him away. He'd reckoned without Morris, of course. He and Harrison were obviously behind the whole ramp from the beginning. It was Renfrew who discovered you were taking an interest."

"Yes," said Dawlish. "And Harrison made a point of buying Tim Jeremy a drink at the club, and so opening a door if we wanted specialized insurance advance. Clever."

"He felt sure he could fool us, but was worried in case you took an unconventional line and stirred the dirt up," Trivett went on. "That would explain why he made trouble for you. Probably his sole purpose was to keep you away from the main theme. Renfrew offered to work with you, to fool you more easily; when you turned him down, he had to distract you some other way."

"I see."

145

"It's clear as it can be," Trivett went on. "Kate Rossitter—or Harrison—knew her father was in it up to the neck, wanted to save him, believed that Renfrew was really responsible. So she set her cap at Renfrew, and did a good job—persuading him that she was ready to take shares in any racket, no matter how crooked. I doubt if you'd have got here in time, and fixed all this, if she hadn't helped."

"So do I," said Dawlish, warmly. "Lovely Kate! She even interceded for poor old Jeremiah Kittle. You haven't forgotten him, by any chance, have you?"

"He was a second string to Harrison's plans," said Trivett. "Harrison knew that there'd probably be suspicion about the way Sir Mortimer Kittle had died, and wanted to pin that on Jeremiah, who had a reasonable motive. Then he saw another way of making millions—frightening the life out of Jeremiah and making him sign documents which would have given him, Harrison, control of his millions. Jeremiah's upstairs—did you know?"

"Oh, yes, I knew."

"He'll be all right," Trivett said. "It's all over, Pat. Hardly any shouting to do."

Dawlish said mildly:

"Bless all policemen, they've such tidy minds."

"What's on yours?" demanded Trivett.

Dawlish chuckled. "Dark suspicions that you don't believe a word—or not many words—of what you've been saying."

Trivett said, "Well, put me right."

"Why did Kate come to see me? Who sent Tim's body in a coffin?"

"Renfrew, of course. And Renfrew, playing on Kate's fears for her father, told her you wanted to see her."

"And drugged her—or taught her how to look as if she had been drugged," said Dawlish. "Then she had a telephone call and came posthaste up here. Convincing?"

"Why not?" asked Trivett. "Once you grant that she was doing her damnedest to beat Renfrew and save her father from his own crookery, that fits in. Dean worked with her, of course. One of our troubles was the fact that Midlon was undoubtedly a genuinely respectable firm. It was the man known as Rossitter, their northern agent, who caused the trouble."

"There I'm in part agreement," said Dawlish. "The villain is Rossitter. Plus Kate."

"Prove it," said Trivett. "Now that Rossitter's dead—"

"Who said he was dead?" asked Dawlish, mildly.

Trivett said, "What you need is a drink, Pat. You saw Harrison's body. I saw the body. It'll soon be on the way to the morgue."

"Identified by Dean and Kate as Rossitter."

"His own daughter—"

Dawlish chuckled. "All right, Bill, call me crazy, but indulge me this far, will you? I want to talk to Kate in front of Jeremiah. I wouldn't object to Prudence Lorne being present, either. I think we might find out the whole truth, which isn't quite what you pretend to think. Just at the moment, Kate has managed to build up her case so well that even if you charged her, she wouldn't be convicted."

"There's no case against her," Trivett said obstinately.

"Will you try it my way, by confronting Prudence and Kate with old Jeremiah?"

"I suppose it can do no harm," said Trivett, reluctantly.

28

Shortcut to Millions

Jeremiah was fully dressed when they went upstairs, and sitting in an armchair. A police officer was with him, and a breakfast tray was by his side. He started up at the appearance of Dawlish and Trivett, then saw Prudence. He jumped out of his chair and rushed toward her, enfolding her in his arms.

"Prudence, my dear, how wonderful to see you!" There were tears in his eyes. "I've been so worried about you and your Aunt May. How is she?"

"Quite all right," Prudence said, her eyes glistening. "You're really—not hurt?"

"No, my dear, mercifully I was spared physical suffering, but the strain—well, if it hadn't been for—"

He broke off.

Kate came into the room, and at the sight of her, Jeremiah dropped his arms from Pru and turned toward the other girl. She smiled at him demurely.

"Miss Rossitter! I'm delighted to see you! I've told Mr. Dawlish what a wonderful help you've been. I—" he broke off again, and his smile faded. "My dear, what does all this mean? These are policemen, aren't they? Your father—"

"He's dead," Dawlish said brutally.

"Dead! Oh, my poor Kate—"

148

Kate said slowly, "Don't talk about it, Mr. Kittle. I'm happier to know he's dead than to think he would have to stand trial. That would have been unbearable." Her voice broke.

"I'm so sorry," said Jeremiah. "So very sorry."

"Anderson killed him," Kate said.

"That man from Safeguard? You know I never liked him," said Jeremiah. "There was something so cold, so inhuman about him. Well, if it's all for the best—" he broke off, shaking his head sorrowfully. "What a tragic business it has been. I know, of course, that your father realized that he couldn't hope to keep free of the police much longer. His attempt to swindle Midlon and the insurance companies was bound to fail; nemesis was creeping up on him. So he killed my poor cousin, and hoped that he could force me to part with most of my inheritance. Shocking, shocking, but—forgive me, my dear young lady, forgive me for saying anything that would be hurtful to you."

Kate didn't speak.

Dawlish said, "I will now tell you all a funny story."

There was a startled silence. Jeremiah's lips parted; he closed them again, and patted the back of Kate's hand. Felicity and Ted appeared in the doorway.

"A very funny story," said Dawlish. "Rossitter isn't dead."

"Pat—" began Trivett, and stopped.

Jeremiah dropped Kate's hand abruptly, and turned to him with angry dignity.

"Mr. Dawlish, kindly stop making a joke of a very real tragedy. Rossitter—"

"Isn't dead," said Dawlish. "He wasn't Harrison. Harrison was in the racket certainly, but not as Rossitter. Kate knows that and so does Dean. All the Midlon directors were in the racket. Midlon did a nice job, by fixing those fires and distracting attention from their main theme. They even managed to frame company frauds, a double dose of distraction. They—"

"Will you kindly stop this man from talking in this nonsensical manner," Jeremiah said sharply.

"You must have guessed by now that I take a lot of stopping," said Dawlish. "Three people knew or suspected the whole truth—Kemp, Harrison, and Renfrew or Anderson. That's why they shot Anderson."

Prudence exclaimed, "*Jimmy?* Shot?" It was the first word she'd uttered, and she looked appalled. "He's not dead, is he? He's not—"

"I'm afraid he is, dear child," said Jeremiah. "He was deeply involved, and actually shot—"

Prudence said "Oh," in a weak voice, and moved suddenly to a chair.

"Kemp knew, and died," Dawlish went on. "Harrison knew, and died, Renfrew knew most of it, and was shot. With them out of the way, a beautifully convincing case against them could be built up. The case, of course, was built to hide the truth—that the real aim was to get hold of the Kittle millions. Sir Mortimer Kittle was murdered, simply to get hold of those. But Renfrew-Anderson had made a lot of trouble, and then Sir Mortimer's mother wasn't satisfied, and came to me. At all costs, I had to be kept off the right scent, but I had a notion of the obvious conclusion—that this was murder for inheritance, and all the rest was a side issue, built to blot out the truth."

"Ridiculous!" cried Jeremiah.

"Fact," said Dawlish. "You see, Jeremiah, I wasn't convinced that we knew the truth about you. Your frequent trips away from home didn't fit in with the life of a struggling insurance agent. I wondered if you had a second identity, nicely tucked away somewhere—an identity which could be lost, or taken off like a cloak, once you inherited the Kittle millions. Prudence!"

Prudence started.

"You suspected that Jeremiah had a mistress in Manchester, didn't you?"

"Prudence!" gasped Jeremiah. "Please—"

Prudence said faintly, "I was afraid of it. I found a lipstick in his pocket one day, and—"

"It is a lie!" cried Jeremiah.

"It's why you tried to have Prudence killed," Dawlish said. "You were reluctant to do so, but had to try. The whole truth is, of course, that you're Kittle alias Rossitter. It suited you to have a mousy little woman like Aunt May fussing and coddling you, prepared to swear that there wasn't a kinder man in all England."

Jeremiah said thinly, "That is a damnable lie. A fantastic accusation. Why—"

"We've had enough of the heartbreak stuff," said Dawlish. "Kate did it so prettily, she almost managed to win over my hard-headed wife. In fact, as your mistress—"

"You must be mad!" gasped Jeremiah.

Kate began to laugh. She threw her head back and laughed lightly at first, then with increasing wildness. She shook from head to foot.

Then suddenly she stopped, and pointed to Jeremiah.

"Look!" she cried. "Look at him! Can you imagine me being anything to poor old Jeremiah? Can you?"

"You'd do a lot for a million pounds," said Dawlish. "The two of you and Harrison fixed it from A to Z. The murder of Sir Mortimer, the Midlon and Safeguard diversions, the distractions for me, the death of the people who knew the whole truth. Kemp—"

"*Is* Kemp dead?" asked Kate, in a quivery voice, as if she would burst out laughing again.

"Didn't you know? Jeremiah slipped out and cut his throat tonight. You see, the murderer had to be someone he trusted, because he was awake before he was killed, and in a pretty nervous frame of mind. First I thought it was you, but you couldn't have been there in time. So I banked on Rossitter. The whole problem turned on the identity of Rossitter, and now we know it. The game's up, Jeremiah."

Jeremiah turned to Trivett.

"Have you no control over this man?" he demanded tersely.

"You might look for the knife with which Jeremiah killed Kemp," Dawlish said to Trivett.

"I repeat that this is a rigmarole of untruths," said Jeremiah thinly. "It is a hodgepodge of illogical, hostile accusation, and I will remind Mr. Dawlish that there is such a thing as a law of slander."

"Pat, can you substantiate—" Trivett began.

"He cannot substantiate a word of it," said Jeremiah, with dignity.

Dawlish grinned.

"No? Then Renfrew known as Anderson will be able to do so when he comes round."

Kate flashed a vicious glance at Dawlish.

She said waspishly, "He's dead, I saw—"

"Oh, no, merely a glancing wound. He'll be up and about soon. Too soon for Rossitter, I fear."

At half past seven that evening, Renfrew came to and was rational enough to make a statement. The documents he had found were hidden in the grounds. He had seen the others arrive, and followed them, to find out Rossitter's identity. He had suspected Harrison for some time. That was why he had worked so secretly, giving so little away. It was his presence at Dawlish's visit to the Safeguard offices which had made Harrison tell Dawlish so much. He knew little about Jeremiah Kittle, but had discovered that on the night of his death, Sir Mortimer Kittle had dined tête-à-tête with Kate Rossitter. He'd since discovered that Sir Mortimer's will had been skillfully forged.

At Manchester that night, Renfrew had followed Harrison, who had gone to Kemp's room; Harrison, not Jeremiah, had killed Kemp, because Kemp had discovered Harrison's position with Safeguard.

Harrison had taken some papers out of Kemp's pocket, including a list of names and addresses of the men he hired for his work of violence. After escaping from Dawlish, Renfrew had gone into the grounds, seen the others arrive, and followed them. Dean had shot him and Harrison.

The papers with the names and addresses were found on Dean.

By noon that day, each man had been picked up.

By noon also, Kate, Dean, and Jeremiah had been remanded in custody for eight days, on a technical charge. The truth was out. Dean had arranged for Tim's capture, and the ghoulish coffin trick, in order to frighten Dawlish off the case, while Jeremiah Kittle, by pretending to be locked in as a prisoner, had tried to keep himself in the clear.

Ten days later, Trivett came into the Hay Mews flat, brisk and businesslike, sporting a new tie.

"Look at him," said Dawlish. "Anyone would think he'd never made a mistake in his life."

Trivett grinned amiably.

"That's right, gloat," he said. "You ought to be grateful that I made things so easy for you."

"How like a policeman," Felicity murmured.

"How's Renfrew?" asked Dawlish, getting out drinks.

"Much improved," said Trivett. "He's still at the Manchester Hospital, making giant strides forward after every visit from Prudence Lorne. That looks like a case. She's probably found the human being underneath that ice of his."

"And Aunt May?"

"The last time I saw her, she looked ten years younger," Trivett said. "Women are never as simple as you think they are." He paused a moment, and then went on: "Well, it's all sewn up now, Pat. We've the evidence that Kate *did* dine with Mortimer Kittle the night before he died, and poisoned him. Also that Midlon and Harrison had been working a racket for years. Dean and Jeremiah were accessories to it, and to Kemp's murder. How's Tim Jeremy?"

"Mending nicely; he's coming to convalesce with us at Haslemere. We collect him from the hospital this afternoon."

"So all's well that end's well."

"If you say so," said Dawlish mischievously.

"I do say so, with very deep respect and er—er—*gratitude* for that nose of yours!" said Trivett, clapping him on the shoulder.